All rights reserved. No part of this book may be reproduced in any form by any electronic or mechanical means including photocopying, recording, or information storage and retrieval without permission in writing from the author.

In the Stars
Paperback Copyright © 2022 Lorhainne Ekelund
Editor: Talia Leduc

All rights reserved.
ISBN-13: 978-1990590467

Give feedback on the book at:
lorhainneeckhart@hotmail.com

Twitter: @LEckhart
Facebook: AuthorLorhainneEckhart

Printed in the U.S.A

IN THE STARS

The Friessens

LORHAINNE ECKHART

The Outsider Series

The Forgotten Child (Brad and Emily)
A Baby and a Wedding
Fallen Hero (Andy, Jed, and Diana)
The Search
The Awakening (Andy and Laura)
Secrets (Jed and Diana)
Runaway (Andy and Laura)
Overdue
The Unexpected Storm (Neil and Candy)
The Wedding (Neil and Candy)

The Friessens: A New Beginning

The Deadline (Andy and Laura)
The Price to Love (Neil and Candy)
A Different Kind of Love (Brad and Emily)
A Vow of Love, A Friessen Family Christmas

The Friessens

The Reunion
The Bloodline (Andy & Laura)
The Promise (Diana & Jed)

The Friessen Family

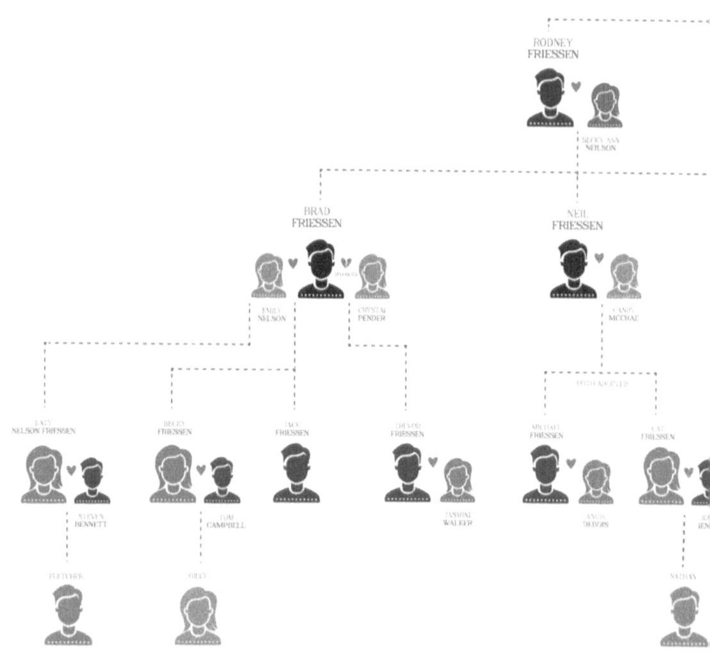

The Outsider Series

THE FORGOTTEN CHILD	BRAD & EMILY
A BABY AND A WEDDING	BRAD & EMILY &
FALLEN HERO	JED, DIANA & ANDY
THE SEARCH	JED, DIANA & ANDY
THE AWAKENING	ANDY & LAURA

The Outsider Series

SECRETS	DIANA & JED
RUNAWAY	ANDY & LAURA
OVERDUE	JED & DIANA
THE UNEXPECTED STORM	NEIL & CANDY
THE WEDDING	NEIL & CANDY

The Friessens
A New Beginning

THE DEADLINE	ANDY & LAURA
THE PRICE TO LOVE	NEIL & CANDY
A DIFFERENT KIND OF LOVE	BRAD & EMILY
A VOW OF LOVE,	THE ENTIRE
A FRIESSEN FAMILY CHRISTMAS	FRIESSEN FAMILY

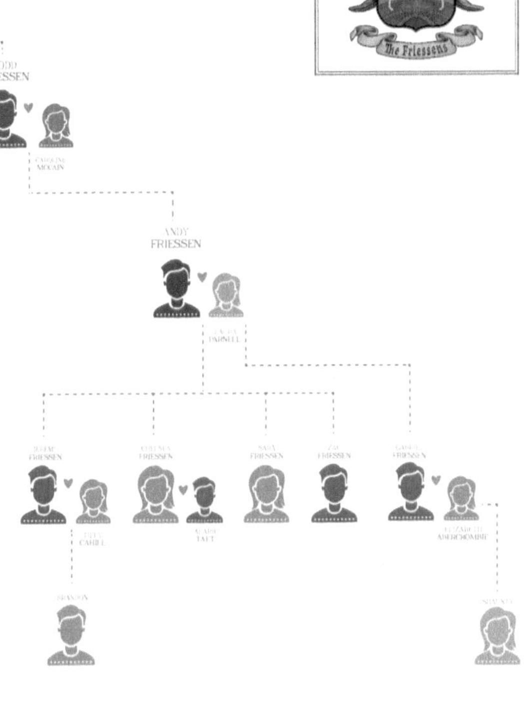

The Friessens

LEAVE THE LIGHT ON	KATY & STEVEN
IN THE MOMENT	BECKY & TOM
IN THE FAMILY	THE ENTIRE FRIESSEN FAMILY
IN THE SILENCE	CAT & XANDER
IN THE STARS	DANNY & EVIE
IN THE CHARM	CHRIS & ED
UNEXPECTED CONSEQUENCES	CHRIS & ED

The Friessens

IT WAS ALWAYS YOU	KATY & STEVEN
THE FIRST TIME I SAW YOU	GABRIEL & ELIZABETH
WELCOME TO MY ARMS	CHELSEA & ALARIC
WELCOME TO BOSTON	PAIGE & MORGAN
I'LL ALWAYS LOVE YOU	JEREMY
GROUND RULES	JEREMY & TIFFY
A REASON TO BREATHE	TREVOR & JASMINE
YOU ARE MY EVERYTHING	MICHAEL & ANGIE
ANYTHING FOR YOU	
THE HOMECOMING	THE ENTIRE FRIESSEN FAMILY

Don't ever fall in love with your best friend!

Join a brand new generation of Friessens in *New York Times* and *USA Today* bestselling author Lorhainne Eckhart's Friessen Family series. In the latest volume, two lifelong friends don't realize their love for each other.

Evie and Danny have been friends forever, and neither has considered the other in a romantic way. Then, one day, in drives Charlie Adams, the sexy, gorgeous daughter of the town banker. When she sets her sights on Danny, he just can't resist her charms.

Little does he know, Evie is about as down and out as she can get, working a dead-end job, with less than twenty dollars in her bank account. Her future and options are bleak, and to make it worse, as she watches from the sidelines, she realizes she has loved Danny forever.

Will Danny realize that the love of his life may not be the woman he's dating?

— "Love love love this series! Quick fun reads about a family you'll become obsessed with!"

K. Orost

— "I know when I pick up one of Ms. Eckhart's books that I will laugh, cry, feel the romance and totally be entertained!"

Jubare

— "Is it possible for a friend of seventeen years to bcome a lover? Another riveting family book from the gifted Lorhainne Eckhart."

C. Crain

D anny Friessen was most known for his brilliant red hair and vibrant blue eyes, which were gifts from his mother, Diana Friessen, and for his stubborn "go it alone" attitude, which he'd apparently inherited from his father—that and the same difficult and intense characteristics that gave him his focus and drive as well as his tendency to be unreasonable at times, as his mother had informed him. His father had only laughed and said, "That's my boy," especially considering Danny resembled him more and more every day.

His friends at school often looked to Danny to lead them, but he chose to be the silent observer instead of the life of the party. That had earned him the nickname Mr. Mysterious, and he rightly couldn't remember whether it had been the popular girls, the jocks, or the student council who'd labeled him as such in the graduation yearbook three years earlier.

"So watcha doing?"

Danny hadn't heard her pull up. Evie Wetzel was short, slim, with mud-brown eyes and dark hair that was always tied back in a ponytail. Her silent arrival was a surprise, considering her muffler was shot and her tailpipe was secured with wire from a coat hanger, but sure enough, there was her rusty brown pickup parked by his older Bronco.

"Hope you don't mind me dropping by?" she said.

Danny just shook his head. "Of course not."

Evie seemed to always wear the same faded blue jeans and sleeveless plaid shirt. They'd been friends since Mrs. Friedman's kindergarten class, where he'd perpetually been a thorn in the uptight woman's side. He still remembered standing beside his mother as she was informed of his unacceptable, rambunctious, out of control behavior after he'd refused to sit still and listen, then gone on to make farting noises behind the teacher's back and raid the stash of M&M's in her drawer.

"Just cleaning up all this tack and oiling these bridles for my dad," Danny said. "Why don't you get your ass in here and help me?"

Evie worked for her own dad, a former butcher, who owned the Tasty Pig, one of the best barbecue stops in the state, as far as Danny was concerned. He tossed her a pair of work gloves from the bin beside the tack room, which she caught one handed as she strode over. He worked oil into a cracked bridle that was part of the gear his dad used for the horses. Jed Friessen was a cowboy to the core, as his mom teased, with his love of horses. He was still taking groups out for day and overnight trips on horseback, teaching kids to connect with the animals.

"So what brings you by?" Danny said. "Would've thought you'd be working, or is it that late already?" He didn't have a clue what time it was, since it was Saturday and he'd just come back from an hour's ride after studying his prelaw courses all morning until his brain was fried. The ride always gave him a chance to decompress and figure out a lot.

"Closed up early today," Evie said. "Dad's been losing business, competing with that new chain restaurant that opened up right next door, so I thought I'd come by and bug you." She worked in the oil like a pro, but then, Evie had grown up much like him but with two sisters instead, both older. She shared his love of horses, considering her dad had a small acreage with two of his own as well as some chickens and goats.

"That sucks," Danny said. "People gotta know there's no question on who's better. They'll figure it out." He wondered, though, as he'd known for a while that her dad's place wasn't quite the hit it should've been.

She just shrugged. "Well, seems many disagree, wanting three pages of the same old mediocre variety compared to Dad's barbecue. They don't get that he knows meat better than anyone in the county. If it keeps up, Dad is talking about cutting back on my hours—but enough about my woes, since this should teach me to get up off my heinie and figure out something else. Do you think I'd have a chance as an airline stewardess, jet setting off to all kinds of exotic locations?" She stared up at him, and the expression on her face was priceless as she batted her lashes.

Danny took her in. At five one or two, tops, she was tiny. He could picture those in the trade, and he just couldn't see her in one of those pantsuits or skirts. All he could imagine was her smart mouth as she jumped up to try to reach the overheads and tossed old guys bags of nuts. He had to shake his head before she nudged him, gave him a haughty smile, and winked, showing her bottom two teeth, crooked, the same slight crossover she'd had since they were kids.

"I'm kidding," she said. "Geez, you should see your face. You know, you could at least pretend that I'd rock at it."

"You want me to lie?" he said and took a poke in the ribs from her.

"Hey, seriously, be nice!" she replied.

He had to laugh. "You know you can be anything you want. Maybe it's time for you to figure out what you want to do, go back to school…"

She was already shaking her head. "I'm not the brainiac you are. You know that. I barely passed high school. You know how I struggled with every class, including gym, which I failed miserably. I was the one who never got picked for anything, as I couldn't run, catch, or fetch. With my grades, a scholarship was never in the cards, and you know my parents didn't have savings put away for postsecondary. I suppose I could get a student loan, but then, I don't have a clue for what, so, all in all, seems kind of a waste of time and money, don't you think? And don't suggest prelaw like you," she added.

Danny took in her big eyes, the humor that was always poking him, and the fact that she'd never let a moment slip without pointing out how smart he was. The fact was that school and learning came easy for him, always had, but he remembered how painful school had been for Evie. Everything he aced, she struggled to get, but every smart-mouthed comment she dished out had been a source of amusement for him.

"Yeah, but you have the skill of managing idiots," Danny said. "That alone should get you…" He stopped and took in the way she was staring at him. "Come on, Evie. Seriously, even in school you were always quick with a comeback and a dash of sarcasm. You'd be great in anything dealing with people."

She sighed as she hung up the oiled bridle and reached in the bin to grab another. "Well, you ever thought that maybe I'm not comfortable in front of people? I'm just not willing to ignore and excuse idiotic behavior like everyone else does."

Just then, he heard a car, and he glanced back to take in his dad's pickup, shiny, black, and fairly new. He watched as his mom and dad got out. He could hear them talking, laughing.

"Hey, Evie," his mom called out and waved.

"Hi, Mrs. Friessen."

He knew his mom had always liked Evie, having often pulled her aside for tea when she and Danny were kids. His dad had teased it was the closest his mom would get to having a daughter—not that there was anything between Danny and Evie. There never would be. She was his friend, and that was all he saw her as, and she him.

"Evie, I see Danny roped you into helping clean the tack," His dad said as he stepped into the barn. His dark hair was short, and he pressed his cowboy hat to his head. His jeans were new and clean, and his gray T-shirt pulled at his wide chest. His dad's barn now had eight stalls and was heated, with an enclosed riding ring and viewing room parents could sit in to watch after they dropped off their kids.

"Ah, you know I don't mind," Evie replied. Danny took in the way his dad was watching him and then her.

"You two heading out for a ride today?" His dad asked. Danny knew his dad would've loved to saddle up and take off into the hills, but his mom had roped him into errands with her, and then there was the chore of looking after his brothers, Mark and Christopher, both off doing he didn't have a clue what.

"Just got back from one when Evie drove in," Danny said just as he heard music and another car. The music grew louder as a red flashy Mustang GT convertible pulled in beside Evie's truck, dust spewing. The horses started kicking up in their stalls from the jarring thump of the bass, and the ones out in the corral were racing around.

"Who the hell…?" His dad started just as the car turned off, and so did the music.

Out stepped Charlene Adams, Charlie for short. She was tall and leggy, with long, sleek black hair, dressed in a pink crop shirt that showed off her belly button ring. She could have graced the cover of any magazine, and she had a smile that dazzled.

He heard Evie utter a crude remark.

"Hey, Danny," Charlie said, stepping into the barn in sandals with a slight heel, her toes painted red. She lifted her dark shades, shoving them on top of her head. "Oh, hey there, Evie. Didn't know you were here. Was wondering whose pickup that was. Thought it might be one of the hired hands."

"Nope, just mine," Evie said. "It may not look like much, but it runs. Hey, you may want to be careful of that pile of manure. You wouldn't want to wreck that pedicure."

Charlie stopped and stared at the pile of horse dung Danny hadn't yet cleaned up since brushing down his speckled gray gelding and putting him in his stall with a fleck of hay. His dad rubbed the back of his neck, and he was expecting him to say something.

"Hi, Charlie," Danny finally said. "What are you doing out here?" He could feel his dad staring at him, and he glanced over, taking in his expression and almost hearing him say, *Seriously?*

"Thought I could interest you in a movie tonight, maybe dinner first," she said and smiled, showing perfectly straight white teeth. It was one of those smiles that seemed to start at her toes and move all the way through her. Some people could pull off that magic with just a smile, and Charlie was one of them.

A horse knickered, and another kicked at the stall, still unsettled. He noticed the way Charlie stiffened.

"They're likely spooked from the way you blew in here, music cranked and all. Loud noise and craziness doesn't mix with horses," Evie said, and Danny picked up her dripping sarcasm.

"Sorry about that!" Charlie shrugged and smiled again, then looked around, setting her eyes on his dad, who was still leaning against the wall, taking them in. "Oh, you must be Danny's father. Wow, now I see where he gets his looks from!" Charlie actually held out her hand to his dad, and he wasn't sure what Evie muttered under her breath, but he was sure it wasn't anything a lady should say.

His dad took her hand. "Charlie," he said, glancing at Danny. "Charlie's kind of an unusual name for a girl."

She slid her hands in her back pockets, which only

accentuated her perfectly rounded breasts. "Mom's sense of humor. Dad wanted a son but got me instead, so Charlene turned into Charlie, and it stuck." She was giving that megawatt smile to his dad, and he took in Evie rolling her eyes behind her. He wanted to shake his head for her to stop before his dad slapped his arm.

"Well, I'm sure your mother has some things lined up for me to do, so I'll let you kids finish up here. Oh, Danny, can you also make sure to clean up the saddles, too? I've got a group coming in Wednesday." Then his dad wandered out and stopped in front of the cherry red Mustang, taking it in before shaking his head as he kept going.

"So how 'bout it?" Charlie asked. She stood at least six inches over Evie. "Can I interest you in taking a break and going with little ol' me to a movie and maybe a bite to eat tonight? Oh, and before I forget, I wanted to tell you I was telling my dad about you being in prelaw, and he said he's got a friend he'd love to introduce you to. He sold his big Chicago firm and settled out here to open an office in Arlington. He's a pretty big name, litigating some of the biggest cases back east, and he's now trying to keep a low profile, but he's coming for dinner tomorrow night, so how about joining us and meeting him? It would be great to have that contact and resource." Charlie was so vibrant, a looker. She'd been on the arm of one jock or another all through high school and college. He was still surprised she'd stuck close to home, opting to go to the same community college he did. What that was about, he didn't have a clue.

"Yeah, I don't know," he said. "I've got some more studying to do…"

"Ah, come on," Charlie said. "All work and no play, you know the saying. Come on, Evie. You can join us, too. Tell Mr. Mysterious to loosen up and come have some fun." She tossed Evie a glance over her shoulder, then slid her hand over his bicep. "You'll have fun, and hey, I promise no chick flick. You get to pick whatever macho blood and guts movie you want."

Her hands were soft, and there was something about her persistence and the way she touched him that had him considering her proposal. Maybe she knew she was getting somewhere, as she slid her arms around his waist and hugged him.

"Please, Danny, pretty please?"

Yup, she was all soft and warm, and damn, she smelled good.

"Okay, fine," he said. As Charlie looped both her arms around his neck, he took in shock, he thought, in Evie's eyes. She squeezed the leather of one of the bridles. Just then, Charlie planted a kiss on his lips that went from zero to a hundred. Wow! When he broke the kiss and looked over, Evie was at her truck, door open, lifting her hand to wave.

"Hey, aren't you coming?" he called out. Charlie was still plastered against him, her hand now resting on his chest.

"Nope, not this girl," Evie said. "You, though, have fun. Later!" Then she was in her truck and backing out.

"Well, three's a crowd anyway," Charlie said, and he took in her expression at the rattle and roar of Evie's truck, which was sounding more and more as if it was on its last legs.

Chapter Two

Danny had finished cleaning all the saddles, and Charlie had talked nonstop the entire time about her classes, her dad, her family, and how Chicago was the one place she was destined to live. Where was she now? Waiting for him downstairs, at her insistence, likely perched against her overpriced Mustang, as he showered in the loft above the barn. That was where he lived now, an open-concept suite with a bed, kitchen, living room, and reasonable bath. It gave him privacy and a place of his own, even if it was on his parents' ranch outside North Lakewood.

He turned off the shower and stepped out, then pulled a towel from the rack and dried off. Tying it around his waist, he stepped out barefoot, seeing his unmade bed and clothes tossed in a heap in the corner. He yanked a clean pair of jeans, socks, and underwear from his dresser and tossed them on the bed. He could hear talking from the open door at the bottom of the stairs that led into the barn—Charlie, he thought. Who she was talking to now, he didn't have a clue.

He quickly pulled on a white dress shirt and tucked it in before pulling on a belt and his boots. Then he grabbed his wallet and keys after running his fingers through his short red hair. He jogged down the stairs into the barn and took in the stalls, how neat and tidy everything was, and the box of tools he'd left out.

Charlie was leaning against her Mustang, the phone pressed to her ear, talking away to someone, and then there was his dad, walking his way, taking in the tall, slim, gorgeous, and stacked Charlie. He wasn't sure what his dad was thinking, from the amused expression on his face. Danny quickly tucked the tools back into the tack room and secured the door just as he heard the scrape of his dad's boots on the concrete of the barn floor.

His dad glanced back to Charlie as he approached. "You heading out for the night?"

"Yeah, we're hitting a movie and stopping for something to eat, likely a beer and a burger in town after." That was what he'd planned, anyway, not that he'd shared that last part with Charlie yet.

His dad nodded. "Well, don't be drinking and driving. I know your mom was wondering what was happening with the girl with the Mustang. She's a looker, and your mom says she's the one who's stopped by here a few times. You dating?" His dad tilted his head in her direction, and the question alone seemed odd coming from him. It had his mom written all over it. He took in Charlie again, who was still talking on her cell phone and didn't seem to care whether anyone was listening.

"We're friends, is all," Danny said.

Yeah, right. She'd been chasing him as long as he

could remember in between the other guys she'd dated, but their attraction had never gone past…what? He shrugged. Nothing serious. He enjoyed whatever this was.

His dad ran his hand over Danny's hair and ruffled it a bit. "You'd best get clear, you think? Your mom was saying she thought she's the daughter of that First West banker in town, Perry Adams?"

Danny took Charlie in as she spotted him and said goodbye to whoever she was talking to. She pocketed her phone and started into the barn, that smile pasted to her lips.

"She is," Danny said. Charlie's dad had been running the second largest bank in the area for decades, he thought—but then, Charlie never let a moment pass without fitting that fact into a conversation, as if her father's identity defined who she was.

"You ready?" she asked.

"You finished all the saddles, Danny?" His dad called out over his shoulder as he headed to the back of the barn, past the stalls, to where the gate led out to the paddock.

"Done and put away," he said. That had been without Evie's help, too. It wasn't lost on him how she'd slipped away. He'd call her the next day and find out what it was that'd had her dropping by. He suspected something, as he thought about it now. He had a feeling there was more.

His dad lifted the gate and latched it behind him, walking out to where the horses were in the corral.

"That was Darlene," Charlie said, in his space, so close he could feel her heat. "She said there's a party tonight at Matt's in town, and I was thinking maybe after the movie we could head over. There's a pool there, and…"

He noted that she had somehow steered him, and they were walking to her shiny red Mustang, her hand linked to his arm.

"Not into a party tonight," he said. "Just the movie, and let's grab a bite after. I've got a busy day tomorrow, a pile of studying to do, and…"

She stepped in front of him, giving him pouty lips as she slid her hands up his chest and around him, pressing all her softness against him. Damn, she smelled good. "Please, Danny, it'll be so much fun."

He wondered how many guys that worked on. Probably all of them. The kind of parties her friends frequented may have been fun for her, but watching everyone getting shitfaced wasn't his idea of fun. "Nope, not tonight," he said. "Why don't I follow you to your place, or you can leave your car here and I'll drive?"

The disappointment was there in her expression even though he could see she was trying to hide it as she looked around him to his older blue and white Bronco. It was dusty, with some rust here and there, but it ran, and he liked it, and it was his, bought with his hard-earned cash, not handed to him like her overpriced sports car, gifted by her father.

"But my car is—"

"A little too red and flashy for my taste," Danny replied. He took in her frown, and for a minute he thought she was going to try to convince him, but she surprised him by turning and starting to his Bronco, tossing him a glance over her slender shoulder.

"Well, are you coming?" she said, waiting expectantly.

"Yeah, I am," he said. He walked over to her as she stepped around to the passenger side and again waited for him. He reached around her and opened the door, and she climbed up and in. He closed the door behind her, and as he stepped around the Bronco and slid behind the wheel, she began applying a light shade of lipstick.

He backed up and drove down toward the highway that would lead into town. "So, movie. You sure you're going to be okay with me picking?"

"I did say you can pick. Just hoping whatever you choose has a storyline with not too much blood and guts and blowing everyone up," she teased. "Any ideas yet?"

He could hear her rustle in the passenger seat. Now she was probing and likely trying to steer him in a certain direction, but he already had a movie in mind and would rather wait until they got there to tell her, or maybe he would buy the tickets without revealing it. He'd get her seated in the theater, waiting for the show, and just thinking of the wait making her squirm had a smile tugging at his lips. She wasn't the patient type, and maybe that was why she intrigued him so much.

He shook his head. "We'll see when we get there."

She reached over and tapped his arm. "You're such a tease, Friessen," she said just as they hit the edge of town and turned down past the gas station. Danny could see the new restaurant up ahead on the right, with lights and glitter and what looked like several people going inside.

"Hey, isn't that Evie's pickup?" Charlie said, pointing to a truck at the side of the road across two parking spots in front of the restaurant, hood up, steam coming out.

"Yeah," Danny said. He signaled and pulled over behind it.

"What are you doing?" Charlie asked and glanced to her watch.

"Stopping," he said and jammed the Bronco in park, then turned off the ignition.

"But the movie… We'll be late."

Maybe it was the sharp glance he tossed her way that had her stopping. Seriously?

"Sorry, that was completely selfish," she said.

He raised his brows, and she appeared sheepish and shrugged. Danny yanked the handle on his door and stepped out to Evie's pickup, seeing the steam and what looked like a blown radiator hose as he peeked in. The engine looked to be held together with duct tape and twine. He rolled up the sleeves of his white shirt to the elbows.

"What are you doing?" Charlie appeared beside him, making a face at the steam and hiss, sweeping her hand in front of her face.

"Taking a look. It appears this just happened." He reached in and then pulled his hand back, feeling the burn from the steam. "Shit…"

"Hey, I'm sure she's already headed to the station for a tow. What can you do? Let the professionals handle it, Danny—you know, a mechanic?"

He tossed her another glance before resting his hand on the front of the truck and seeing the tear in the hose. He just needed to get that off, grab another, and fasten it on. "Mechanics cost money, and this looks like an easy fix," he said, turning around and seeing the restaurant just ahead. It was her dad's place. Maybe that was where she was.

"I guess Evie is struggling," Charlie said. "I know her dad's already missed the last two payments on his line of credit. His restaurant isn't producing, and Dad said he thought they were down to just family for staff, since Mr. Wetzel doesn't have the cash flow to cover people's wages."

Danny was leaning on the frame and took in Charlie. "Your dad shares personal banking business with you?" he said. He should probably tell his parents. He knew his dad had an account there, and he did as well. Maybe it was time to look at another bank.

This was the first time he'd ever seen Charlie speechless, as if she was fighting to think of something to explain her faux pas. He saw the moment she realized, as she winced. "Please don't say anything to anyone. I shouldn't have said anything," she said, appearing sheepish. He'd never seen her out of her comfort zone before, caught doing or saying something she shouldn't have.

"No, you're right, you shouldn't have, but it's your dad who was in the wrong. He shouldn't be sharing clients' private information with you or anyone. Not sure how comfortable I am knowing your dad has loose lips." He rested his hand on the rim of the truck, turning and seeing Evie coming out of her dad's restaurant, a jug in one hand and what looked like duct tape in the other.

"So I guess the movie is out," Charlie said, and he heard her sigh beside him.

He saw the moment Evie noticed them, the slight hesitation before she kept walking, and he gazed down to Charlie beside him. "Uh, yeah," he said. "Evie's my friend. I'm not bailing on her."

Charlie shrugged before nudging him teasingly. "I

get it, Friessen. It's probably why I like you so much. You have a soft spot for helping those who need it. It's just… can't you be a knight in shining armor at a time that's a lot more convenient?"

"Knight in shining armor, huh?" he said. He'd never been called that before, and he took in the grin spilling now from Charlie's expression.

"Yeah," she said. "It's just one of your many flaws."

Chapter Three

When it rained, it poured! Seriously, Evie's entire life as of late had become a storm. Her bank account was declining rapidly, and her last stop for twenty dollars at the ATM had left her twelve dollars and thirteen cents, which wasn't going to pay for a new hose. Her truck was parked at the side of the road, two doors down from her dad's barbecue stop, which was currently closed for the night. To make matters worse, it was practically in front of the new chain restaurant, which was nearly packed, and everyone was watching through the window. So, with a roll of duct tape and a jug of water to fill the leaking radiator, she'd figure out some way of patching it up so she could at least get it home and figure something out. This was just one more sign that her heap of rust was one step from the junkyard.

She saw two people standing by her truck, one a guy, the other… Shit, Danny and Charlie! Of all people, why did it have to be them? Evie was itchy and sweaty and tired, and she wanted to go home and climb into the shower and try to forget what a disaster today was turning into.

"You ran into a little trouble here," Danny called out to her just as Charlie smiled brightly and lifted her hand in a wave as if they were the best of friends. Not! They definitely ran in different circles, Charlie fitting the mold of the all-American girl and Evie trying to just fit.

"What can I say? Thought I'd add some entertainment to the area, breaking down in front of the new chain, just adding some humility to my day." She took in the smile from Danny. The blue of his eyes had only gotten better with age. He was shaking his head. "So have you stopped to help, or is this just…?"

Danny took in what she was carrying. "I can understand the water, but not sure the duct tape is gonna work here," he said. "Took a look at that hose, and it's likely beyond repair." He actually took the duct tape from her hand and rested it on the lip of the truck. She could see he already had grease smudged on his forearm and the edge of his white shirt. Then there was Charlie standing there.

"Didn't you know there's nothing duct tape won't fix?" Evie said. "Just put enough on there and it'll hold it together to get me home. Aren't you two on your way to a movie?"

A date, actually. She'd seen how Charlie had set her eyes on Danny the moment she'd pulled in that afternoon, but then, she'd always had a thing for him, whispering it in the halls of school and to Evie time and again when she was between guys. Evie'd just thought Danny had enough smarts not to fall for all that flash, glitz, and a pretty face. Guess he was just like every other guy.

"What kind of friend drives right on by and doesn't stop to help? You got an old rag, a wrench?" He was leaning in her truck engine again, touching the steaming hose. He pulled his hand back and shook it off as he hissed. "Yup, way too hot to touch right now."

"I got a pair of work gloves in back, plyers in the glove box," she said.

Danny walked around her, leaving her standing by the open hood of her truck with Charlie. She glanced over to where he was pulling open the back of his Bronco.

"Danny saw you broke down and wouldn't drive away and leave you," Charlie said. "He's quite the guy. Chivalry seems to have missed most, but Danny's brought it back—kind of like he's the last of a dying breed of men who know how to be men."

Evie just stared at Charlie, stunned. She'd always figured, with her looks, she was more airhead than brains. Then Danny was back with an old rusty toolkit. He dropped it on the ground and grabbed an old pair of work gloves from it, then set to work figuring out how to fix the unfixable. With a greasy rag, he wiped the hose, and she found herself just watching his focus.

"Evie, rip off a strip of duct tape and hand it to me. Let's hope it holds enough to move the truck."

She pulled at a length of the heavy gray tape and used her teeth to rip it, then took in the intense gaze leveled her way as she handed it to him. He'd been her friend since they were kids, but he was a man now, handsome, with strength in his forearms, broad shoulders, narrow waist, long legs, and even his butt, which she tried not to glance at. She could see why Charlie was chasing him down.

He was wrapping the duct tape around the hose, holding it with one gloved hand, and she knew by the expression on his face that it was hot. "Rip off some more, keep it coming," he said, and thankfully she had something else to focus on.

"You think it will work?" Charlie asked.

"Just a patch job, but enough to get Evie home," Danny said as she bit off another piece and handed it to him. He shook his head at her. "Using your teeth? I can just hear your mother, if not mine, saying dental work is expensive," he teased and then winked.

Now why did he have to do that?

"There, that should hold it," he said, then opened the water reservoir. "You got more antifreeze?" he asked.

Evie just shook her head. "I've got water, which will work just fine."

Danny gestured to the jug and took it from her to pour it in, handling the fix that she could have done easily, but this was the first time it felt as if he were taking care of her, and she liked it more than she should have. Instead of feeling good, she felt alone, and she didn't understand why, not really. His romantic interest would be played by Charlie, the all-American hot babe, who had everything—including the guy Evie had never allowed herself to think of as more than a friend.

"Okay, that should take care of it," Danny said. "Climb in, start it up, and I'll follow you to your place." He closed the hood and tucked the tools and gloves in his kit.

"Thanks, Danny, but it's likely good. I wouldn't want you two to miss the movie, so why don't you…?"

Danny was shaking his head. "It's just a movie, Evie. There'll be another," he said, glancing down to Charlie, who was now standing closer to him than before, resting her slender hand with its red painted nails on his arm and rubbing.

"Danny's right," she said. "Don't be silly, Evie. We'll just go to the movies another night." She smiled up at him, and it wasn't lost on Evie that she was saying exactly what he wanted to hear. How was it that this kind of flirting came so naturally to some and had completely left Evie?

Danny was holding out his hand. For what, she didn't have a clue, and she wondered whether her expression showed how rattled she was. "Keys, Evie," he said. "On second thought, I'll drive your truck. You can follow in the Bronco with Charlie."

She slid her hand in her pocket and pulled out her keys. "You don't need to drive my truck," she said, but at the same time, as all the townspeople were still gawking at her broken-down truck, she wanted to breathe a little easier knowing Danny would take it off her.

He took her keys, pressing his into her hand and leaning closer. "Yeah, I do," he said, then glanced back to the people watching. He knew. Damn him for being so sensitive!

Then he was walking back to his Bronco and tucking his toolkit in back. As he got into her truck, she was seeing Danny in a way she never had before.

She was still holding the jug and tape, and she tossed them in the flatbed of her truck, where the old spare tire was, before walking on shaky legs to the driver's side of his Bronco and climbing in. She searched for the lever to slide the seat all the way forward, and it wasn't lost on her that she could barely see over the wheel. Yeah, Danny was tall, and his Bronco was made for a tall guy.

"Isn't Danny amazing?" Charlie said as she closed the passenger door and pulled on her seatbelt.

Evie started the Bronco, sitting up as straight as she could, seeing Danny already driving away and turning right. "Guess that's why we've been friends since forever," she said. She'd never driven his Bronco before, and she was surprised, frankly, that she was behind the wheel now. She jammed the brakes a little too hard at the stop sign, and the tires squealed, jerking it to a stop. "Go figure, he's got good brakes," she muttered. That meant she likely needed new brake pads or something.

She couldn't help the unfamiliar nervousness that had crept into her, maybe because this was the first time she was in a confined space with one of the popular girls she was pretty sure had looked down her nose at her all her life. She was damn uncomfortable, especially as she could see Danny way in the distance, now turning down the side road that led to her parents' small acreage, where she still lived. A lack of funds meant a lack of choices, another reason she needed to figure out a lot of things rather quickly.

"You're lucky to have a friend like that," Charlie said. "Can honestly say he kind of surprised me when he pulled that knight in shining armor thing, needing to make sure you were okay, and then not just driving away. Honestly, it was the first time I ever experienced that kind of thing. It's damn attractive, which is why I can't figure out why Danny doesn't have a steady girlfriend. I have to say I'm very happy about that, though.

It's as if fate is on my side, and the stars have all aligned. You know, like when you meet that guy you know is the one, and just being near him takes your breath away and makes you want to do everything he wants, no questions asked? He's so dreamy, and I've never felt this way before. Is this love?"

Evie nearly missed the turn as she glanced in horror at Charlie. Why was it some girls needed to spill everything they were thinking and feeling? Talking about Danny this way wasn't helping.

"You know, you should come with us tonight," Charlie said. "We were going to eat after the movie, but let's just go someplace and have a bite, the three of us."

The way she said it, it was as if they were the best of friends. She wasn't being a snob or stuck up, and for a minute Evie was trying to remember why she didn't like her.

She could see that her dad was home, his old Buick parked in front. It had seen better days, and she cringed, driving in. Danny hadn't been there in a long time, and Charlie never. There was something about how old and rundown her home was that had her wanting to keep everyone away instead of letting them have a glimpse into her life.

"Yeah, not tonight," Evie said. "I've got a truck to repair."

With only twenty dollars and a few cents in her wallet, there wasn't a chance in hell she was going to tag along and waste the little money she had left eating in town when there was a perfectly good loaf of bread inside and a can of tuna with her name on it. Any restaurant was a luxury she couldn't afford, though that was something she had no intention of sharing.

As she parked the Bronco, she saw her dad outside in front of her truck, talking with Danny.

"Well, you go, girl—but it would've been my treat," Charlie said. This time Evie looked over at her, and whatever was in her expression seemed far too much like pity.

Chapter Four

He'd seen Charlie on campus all week, running into her at every turn, outside classes and in the hall. Today, after a hellish week, he found her waiting for him, leaning against his Bronco in a pair of jeans and a midnight blue silky tank, her long dark hair hiked up in a messy bun. She was radiant and smiled teasingly as she slid her dark glasses down her nose to peer at him before slipping them on top of her head. The entire motion was sexy, so much like a drug that had him feeling lighter after a crappy day in his last class. The visiting professor took the terms "difficult" and "uncommunicative" to a whole new level.

"Well, you're a sight," he said, walking over to the Bronco and shoving the key in the lock. He tucked his old leather case with his books, notes, and laptop behind his seat and then pushed the heavy door closed.

"You too," she said. "So it's Friday. How about that rain check?"

He didn't say anything as he stepped closer to her. Her body seemed to move toward him as her head tilted up. She was giving everything to him in that smile, her perfect body, and her hand rested on his chest and moved lower, over the flat of his stomach, a gesture that was so teasing and had him covering her hand with his.

"What do you mean by rain check?" he said, and she leaned in closer, going up on her tiptoes and pressing a kiss to his lips. She was the perfect height, leggy and tall, but he was still a head taller.

"You know, the movie we didn't get to see last weekend? Not that I'm complaining. It was nice of you, the way you insisted on following Evie home, helping her out."

He remembered how Evie's dad, Bill Wetzel, had pulled in just ahead of him at their home on the other side of North Lakewood, two acres with a double wide that had seen better days. It wasn't lost on him the way Bill had taken in Charlie before thanking Danny. He wasn't sure what it was about her that had caught his eye, maybe her stature. At the same time, she hadn't thumbed her nose at their downward turn in fortune. Even he could see from everything about their place that they were struggling. He really should give Evie a call.

"She's my friend. It wasn't even a question. So you're not upset about skipping dinner, either?" he said. He'd basically driven them back to the ranch after, where Charlie had surprised him by pressing a kiss to his lips that was tender and had left him wanting more. Then she'd slid behind the wheel of her Mustang and driven away.

"Of course I am, but I completely understand why," she said. Okay, there she went, saying all the right things. Her hands were still touching him, and his were skimming her sides over the curves of her breasts, and her smile only widened. "But you can make it up to me."

The way she was looking at him had him lowering his head and taking in her offered lips. They were so pink and full and tasted so good. He allowed the kiss to linger and his hands to roam freely down her back and over her rounded ass, perfection pressed against him. He heard a whistle and a catcall, but he didn't pull away, just held her and finished the kiss. Her shades were perched on her head, and she appeared shy for a minute, running her tongue over where his lips had tasted her.

"You know what? Why don't I swing by around six, pick you up for dinner?" he said, still holding her. Her breasts were pressing against his chest. She was a perfect fit. "First I want to swing by and have a word with Evie," he added.

Charlie stepped back, a bright smile on her face, and he could see her thinking. "Why don't you invite Evie to come out with us? Maybe invite one of your friends and set her up. We'll do like a double date."

The last thing he wanted to do was set Evie up, and he was shaking his head, but she was already pulling her phone from her purse. "Okay, then I will," she said. "Rand would be perfect. Why didn't I think of him? He's not seeing Heather anymore, and I think he kind of had a thing for Evie in school."

Rand Shepperd was just one of those guys who fit in with everyone, not really a jock but not a geek either, just a guy who went with the flow and now worked as a sales rep at his dad's dealership. Danny didn't know him, yet there was Charlie, on the phone as if she had him on speed dial, talking away. He listened to her issue the invite, and then she hung up. "He's in, so…" She poked him in the stomach with her finger. "Your turn. Invite Evie. Let's get her out of the house to have some fun."

"You know, it's really thoughtful of you to think of Evie and want to help, but she may not be interested. Rand, I can tell you right now, isn't someone she would be interested in," he said—not that he knew what her type was. In fact, he couldn't remember her ever having a steady boyfriend.

"Isn't getting Evie out more important?" Charlie said. "How you worry about your friend is a quality that sets you apart from everyone, so let me help. Honestly, what will it hurt? Even if she and Rand don't hit it off, at least we got her out of the house, and Rand is a good guy. You never know, they could actually be exactly what the other needs." She slid her hands up his chest and pressed her lips to his, kissing him again. "Okay?"

Danny took a breath, taking in something in Charlie he'd never seen before. "Fine, but no promises that she'll agree."

Charlie squealed, patting his chest. "But you'll convince her, I'm sure. So see you at about quarter to six. Oh, and before I forget, this Sunday, come for dinner. That friend of Daddy's is coming, the lawyer I was telling you about, and he wants to meet you."

Oh, he vaguely remembered her mentioning him. "You're not trying to set something up for me, are you?"

She shrugged as her hands lingered now on his wrists. "I may have just happened to mention a few times that you're the top of your class in prelaw and really focused on your career, and he just happens to have a soft spot for helping up 'n coming young lawyers be the best they can be."

He raised a brow, and he could tell by her expression there was more.

"Okay, he's got connections, so why not use them? Seriously, just come and meet him and say something, please, Danny." She was in his face and pleading, and her passion was oozing.

"No promises, Charlie" was all he said, but she threw her arms around his shoulders as if he'd agreed.

"Oh, you won't regret it," she said.

"Charlie, I never said I'd come for sure," he said, resting his hands on her arms to pull her free, fighting his body's wanting of her.

"Oh, but you will, because I'm very persuasive." She stepped away and then flicked her fingers in a wave, walking over to her car, and Danny couldn't pull his gaze from the sway of her perfectly rounded ass.

Chapter Five

Her phone had been disconnected.

Danny had called and gotten the message "This user is temporarily unavailable." He knew that was the standard discreet way of saying Evie hadn't paid her cell phone bill. Now it was stuck in Danny's head, what Charlie had said about how Bill Wetzel was in financial trouble. Evie's dad's restaurant was her only source of income, and she was the only daughter still living at home. Paige, the oldest, was married down in Oklahoma, and Sky, the middle one, worked for the county and lived over in Arlington.

Danny thought about driving to her house and was about to when he spotted her truck parked downtown not far from the Tasty Pig. He found a spot and pulled in, having to walk past the chain restaurant to get there. It seemed to have a steady flow of people.

He saw Evie through the front glass window, noting the new hours written with a Sharpie over the existing sign. They were now serving lunch only and were closing at four, and it was ten minutes to. He pulled the door open and stepped inside, taking in the long counter and one patron, an older balding guy, eating a plate of ribs at one of the six high round tables.

Evie had her dark hair tied back in a high ponytail and glanced up to him. She was in a plain T-shirt, white with black lettering, and an off-white apron tied around her waist. "Hey there, Danny. Stopping by for some barbecue? Dad's brisket is the special today. Lots left, too," she said.

He could see tiny lines dotting the sides of her eyes. Evie wasn't one to let anything get to her, but today it seemed she wasn't hiding it as well, or maybe he noticed because he knew more than he should about what was going on in her life. He wondered how she'd react if she had any idea.

"Sounds great," he said. "How about the brisket to go for four?"

He'd drop it off for his mom and dad. Hopefully they didn't have dinner started already, but they likely did. There it was, Evie's lovely smile as she called out the order through the window to her dad, whom he knew was in back.

"So the other reason I stopped by is I was wondering if you wanted to go for dinner tonight." He took in surprise or something in her face, then hesitation. "With me and Charlie," he clarified. "We're going out and thought of you joining us." He tapped his fingers on the counter and thought he saw disappointment.

"Oh," she said, and it wasn't lost on Danny how her expression changed. "You know what? The third wheel thing doesn't work for me, so you kids have fun." She actually winked, and he sensed distance. "So why are you ordering brisket if you're going out for dinner?"

"No, for my mom and dad. With my mom now working more, it's the least I can do, and they love your dad's barbecue."

Evie took a cloth and wiped the counter. "Your mom's a good woman. Say hi to your parents for me."

"You know you can come by any time. Mom loves it when you do—but seriously, dinner tonight wouldn't be just the three of us."

Evie leaned on the counter. "Oh?" She propped her elbows there and rested her chin in her hands. The spark wasn't quite there in her brown eyes.

"Rand Shepperd is joining us. It was Charlie's idea for the four of us to go out, and it's on me," he added, knowing that if her cell phone was disconnected, she wouldn't have the spare cash for a night out.

"Rand, seriously? Since when are you friends?"

He raised a brow and shrugged. "We're not, and you know that, but I think Charlie's right: It's about the four of us going out to have some good eats, have some fun," he added.

Evie was staring at him as if he'd lost his mind. "So this thing with you and Charlie, is it serious?"

It was like being in the hot seat. He didn't know how to answer, and he could see how she wasn't smiling but seemed to be trying to figure out what he was thinking. "I don't know. Never expected her to be more than just a pretty face."

"Wow, never expected that from you," Evie said.

Her dad called out from the back, and cartons appeared in the window. Evie bagged up the brisket, which he could smell from there. His mouth was watering. He pulled his wallet from his pocket as she rang it up and was about to use his debit card when he saw the cash only sign, so he pulled out his last fifty dollars. He wondered whether he should mention something about the problem with cash only. Maybe now wasn't the time.

"Thank you," he said. "So what do you say? Should I pick you up at six?"

She was so tiny, and he could see her hesitation. She wasn't the same easy person as Charlie. There was so much to Evie, sensitive, kind, a friend who'd always been in his corner. He could see the minute she was about to say no, and he could see what Charlie had seen: She needed this.

"Not taking no for an answer," he said, "just in case you're trying to figure out a way to say that." He stood up, taking the bag and waving away the change as she went through the dismal cash box, clutching at the six dollars plus tip he'd left for her. He'd have given more if he thought she'd take it, but he knew she had a lot of pride and didn't take handouts from anyone.

She shrugged. "Okay, maybe an evening out would be nice," she said, and he reached over and slapped her shoulder.

"I owe you," he said.

She was right behind him as he walked to the door, and when he turned, he took in something in her expression he hadn't seen before. Whatever it was, it seemed different from the way she'd always looked at him. She forced a smile to her face and, holding the door, changed the open sign to closed.

HE COULD SMELL something cooking as soon as he walked in the front door of his parents' rancher. The

TV was on, and he could hear Mark talking with a friend. They were playing video games, he thought. The noise was coming from the family room at the back of the house, and his dad poked his head out from the kitchen. His hair was a mess, his shirt was untucked from his faded blue jeans, and he was barefoot.

"Danny," his dad said as he stepped out, holding a bag of lettuce. "What you got there?"

"Dinner for you and Mom," Danny said as he set the bag on the table. "Stopped at Evie's dad's, and I wasn't planning on buying anything, but…"

His dad lifted out the cartons, the brisket, the slaw, and the wedged potatoes. "Thoughtful of you, even though your mom started dinner this morning. She made chili, but this will be great to go with it, save me having to put a salad out."

"What will be great?" His mom appeared around the corner from her office in back, glasses perched on top of her deep red hair, which was starting to lighten in places. She had vibrant blue eyes and a smile that warmed all their hearts.

"Danny picked up dinner for us from the Wetzels," His dad said.

His mom smiled, lifted a potato wedge, and bit into it. "Yum, this is great. Grab some plates for all of us. I'm starved!"

"Just for you guys," Danny said. "I've got a date."

His mom and dad exchanged a look.

"With the babe in the hot car?" His dad said, and his mom elbowed him. He laughed.

"Her name's Charlie, Dad. Evie and a guy named Rand are also coming. We're going out for a bite to eat, to have some fun."

His mom and dad were staring at him as if there was more, which, of course, there was.

"I didn't know Evie and Charlie were friends," his mom said, appearing confused.

"They're not. It's just…well, it was Charlie's idea to get Evie out, her being down on her luck and all. It's a nice gesture on her part, considering."

"So Evie isn't dating this guy, Rand? You're kind of setting them up?" his mom asked.

He wasn't sure what he was seeing in her expression—curiosity, maybe, or she wasn't keen on the idea. He wasn't too sure. "Evie isn't dating anyone," he said. "This is all Charlie. She was there with me when we spotted Evie's truck broken down, and her dad's restaurant isn't doing well, either, so she thought…"

"So that's why you bought dinner?" His dad said.

Danny shrugged. "Well, kind of. When I got there to the Tasty Pig, I had to walk past the chain next door, which is booming, but there was just one guy sitting at their place. I wanted to do something. Evie mentioned something last weekend when she came by about her dad cutting back on hours, and I didn't think much of it, but then Charlie mentioned Bill's business is in financial trouble. He can't cover payroll, and the only staff are Evie and her mom." He took in the exchange his mom had with his dad. "I totally forgot to mention that to you, by the way. Then when I called Evie today, her cell phone was disconnected, so it's worse than I thought."

His mom and dad appeared surprised.

"That's not good," His dad said, "but it's even worse that a banker is sharing personal client information with his daughter, who in turn is sharing that same private, confidential…" He didn't finish, just staring at Diana. "We still have our accounts at that branch, don't we?"

His mom shrugged, and Danny could see her unease. "My business account and our joint account," she said.

His dad was staring at Danny as if he'd done something wrong.

"Charlie knows she shouldn't have said anything, Dad. It kind of slipped, but it's not an excuse. She shouldn't have shared what she did, and I told her so, but nevertheless, I'm kind of glad, because now I'm thinking Evie could use some help. Like, Mom, you could use some help around here. As an assistant, Evie would be great, or doing some stuff around the ranch."

Diana leveled sharp blue eyes his way. "I would give Evie a job in a heartbeat if I thought she'd take it, but she's smart, Danny. Don't you think she'll figure out this is some kind of handout? I know Evie well enough, and her mom, too, to know that they wouldn't take kindly to that. Jed, did you know the Wetzels were struggling?"

His dad just ran his hand over his head. "I didn't, but that's not something a man shares with his neighbors, and the fact that Charlie shared banking details with you doesn't sit right with me. That's a private matter. Kind of has me wanting to have a word with Perry about his policies and his responsibilities with confidentiality. Then there's our accounts. It's no one's business what we have."

"Or we could just close our accounts and move to another bank," Diana said.

Danny could see this getting heated to the point that something could backfire for the Wetzels. "Or you could forget I said anything," he added.

His mom levelled another difficult gaze his way. "I've taught you better than that. Gossip and sharing personal information about anyone, especially financial information, is never okay. Maybe Charlie isn't the girl you should be seeing," she said, and Danny didn't miss the way his dad turned a heavy amused gaze her way. "I mean, like, how serious is this?"

Danny just shook his head. He and Charlie were just having fun, right? "We're dating, is all. It's not as if I've asked her to marry me."

Oh, that had his dad looking his way. "You have something to share?" His dad said, and his mom appeared speechless as if worried he was serious.

"No, Dad, nothing to share. I'm in prelaw, going to law school next year. I have plans, and they don't include getting married any time soon," he said, watching as a smile touched his dad's lips and he crossed his arms over his chest.

"Well, you'd best be sure that girl you're dating is on the same page as you," he said.

Diana raised a brow as if she had something to add, but Danny started to back up to the front door.

"This is getting to be way too serious a conversation, so I'm going to go," he said before he could say something else that would have his parents giving him a pile of advice he had no intention of hearing right now. Didn't they get that this was just a few friends getting together, nothing serious?

Chapter Six

R and wasn't an uptight guy, Danny knew. He had light hair that he kept cut short, military style, and he had a great build like a lot of the football players, though he was five inches shorter than Danny. He walked in the front door of Ray's Burger Bar, wearing a tight light blue T-shirt that stretched across his chest. He could see the guy hit the weights hard.

"There he is. Rand…" Charlie sang out over the music that blasted from the jukebox, louder than usual, and she waved from where she sat on one of the four stools at the high round bar counter they'd moved to.

Evie was dressed super casually in blue jeans and a faded green shirt, whereas Charlie was sporting a black silky short skirt that showed her amazing legs, tanned and smooth, and a white tank under a black sheer blouse. Her heels were strappy and black, adding another few inches to her height. She brought class to a place known for its ultra casualness.

"Hey there," Rand said and shook Danny's hand, then took the stool opposite, with both girls in between them. "Charlie, thanks for inviting me—and, Evie, it's been a while." He was polite and had a deep voice. His smile was the practiced one Danny thought he used at the dealership.

Menus were already on the table, and a waitress appeared, setting four glasses of water down. "Can I get you something to drink to start?"

"I'm going to have whatever dark lager you have on tap," Danny said, and he reached for his wallet to show his ID. The waitress just nodded.

"Make that two," Rand said.

Evie just shook her head. "Water works for me."

"Oh, come on, Evie," Charlie said. "Have something. I'll have a hard lemonade. Actually, make it two. Evie, you can have one. Let loose for a bit."

Danny could see how Charlie was pushing a bit, trying way too hard, but Evie said nothing as the waitress walked away after checking all their IDs. He knew she preferred beer to coolers. Why she hadn't said anything, he didn't know. "You really want a cooler over a beer?" he teased.

The look she leveled his way was a little hard to read, and he could see her discomfort. Evie was never one to suffer in silence, so he wondered whether it was the money thing. He'd already told her he was buying and was about to say something again when she lifted her hand and got the waitress's attention. "Cancel one of those coolers and change it to your draft on tap," she said.

"Thatta girl," Danny said.

A minute later, the drinks arrived. They ordered burgers all around, except for Charlie, who insisted on a side salad and a lettuce wrap for a bun. Rand and Evie settled into a comfortable conversation as Charlie slid closer to him, sliding her arm through his.

"See? Admit it, this was a great idea." She had a fantastic smile that seemed to ooze all through her. Sometimes he thought it was practiced, but not today, not now. He knew happy, and he could feel it pressed against him.

He couldn't remember the last time he'd been out with Evie. They normally rode horses together, had a beer at his parents' ranch. Now, seeing her with another guy, smiling and talking, he thought for a minute she wasn't carrying such a weight on her shoulders anymore. "Yeah, it was a good idea," he said and glanced back to Charlie, who was leaning against him. He pressed a kiss to her offered lips and pulled back just a bit. "Sometimes you surprise me," he added, taking in the pure joy that seemed to ooze from the mixed blue of her eyes.

"In a good way, I hope." She pulled her lower lip in between her teeth, and he just smiled at her.

"Yeah, all good."

"So, any more thought about dinner on Sunday? Please say yes." She poured her bottle of overly sweet cooler into a glass as Danny lifted his beer and took a swallow.

He shook his head. "You know, it's a nice gesture on your part, wanting me to meet this lawyer friend of your dad's, but it's not really my thing. I'm more about making it on my own, and it's a bit premature for me. I start law school next year at the University of Washington, and I'm not sure I'm comfortable with being offered some kind of favor, maybe being steered in a direction I'm not comfortable with. You mentioned it last Sunday and now this weekend, and it really sounds more like you're handling my life. Even my parents would never do that." He was shaking his head, and a frown appeared quickly on Charlie's face. She'd gone from pure joy to something that resembled a stubbornness he'd yet to see.

"This entire world runs on who you know, Danny. This is the perfect time to meet the kind of people who make things happen in this world. He carries a lot of weight still in Chicago and can open doors for you that you wouldn't be able to open otherwise. He happens to come for dinner often. He and my dad golf almost every Sunday." She was very distinct in how she spoke with a fire and passion when she really wanted something. "So I beg to differ on timing. You're at the beginning of your career, and summer's coming fast. It really would look great on your resume if you were working in a big law firm in some junior position. Chicago just happens to be—"

"Whoa, stop with this Chicago thing. Is that what this is about? I think you forgot my mom is a lawyer here, and a damn good one. I don't really need some big law firm, so don't push, Charlie," he added as he pulled back a bit, not liking the feeling of being directed. He was beginning to feel as if that was exactly what was happening.

"Danny, that isn't what I meant. Of course I know your mom's a lawyer. I'm just trying to help, is all, and I told you already that Chicago is the one place in the cards for me. I have a plan for the future, and Chicago is a great place for lawyers." She took a breath, and he realized that although Rand was talking and Evie was nodding, she was watching him and taking in everything Charlie was saying.

He sat up straighter, feeling the tension and having to roll his shoulders to break off the anger that was starting to take hold. He didn't like anyone getting in his business, trying to make him think a certain way, or, even worse, doing him a favor. "You know what, Charlie? North Lakewood is also a great place for lawyers, with lots of business. People and folks here need help, too," he said.

She shook her head. "Yeah, but billing costs are likely not even close to what you can make in Chicago."

So this was about money. He picked up a toothpick from the holder in the center of the table and shoved it in his teeth, chewing and staring over to her, seeing the flicker of emotions. He wondered whether she had any idea what she'd implied. "You should be clear on something with me," he said. "It's not about the money. If that's what you're chasing, you've got the wrong guy." He shook his head, letting his meaning sink in.

"I'm sorry," she leaned in and whispered. "I didn't mean to push so much. Daddy always said this is one of my faults that I need to work on, but when I care about someone, I just can't help myself. I want to do everything I can." She shrugged again, and he took in her sheepishness. "Forgive me?" She inched closer, teasing him with a smile.

He lifted his beer and took another drink. "Let's just have a good time, and no more shop talk."

Rand and Evie had slipped away to the small dancefloor and started bopping. Rand had great moves, whereas Evie was more reserved, but a few other couples joined them.

"Hey, let's go," Charlie said and slid her hand over his arm, but he just stared at Evie. She looked like she was having a good time, and Rand pulled her closer when a slow song started.

"Yeah, don't really feel like dancing," he said.

The food arrived just as Rand slid his hand lower on Evie's back, over her belt loop, which was only putting Danny more on edge.

Charlie tapped his shoulder. "What's wrong with you?" she said.

He glanced over to her and took in how she was watching him. Then he looked back at the dance floor, over to Rand and Evie. "Nothing," he said. "Let's just eat."

He made a point of reaching for the salt and dumping it on his fries, doing his best not to watch Rand dancing with Evie. What was it about the guy that he didn't think was good enough for her? His hand was holding her a little too close. Danny squeezed the glass salt shaker before putting it back.

Charlie slowly looked out to the dance floor and back to him. Whatever she was thinking, at least this time she kept it to herself.

Chapter Seven

"You've been quiet for almost this entire ride," Evie said. "Although I'm used to the quiet and deep thinker that you are, I'm thinking there's something else going on with you, since this was your idea last night. Remember what you said as you dropped me off? 'Evie, wouldn't it be great to hit the trail in the morning? Come for a ride.' Here I am, so why don't you spill?"

She squeezed the sides of the dark thoroughbred mare to move her closer to Danny. The horse was one from his dad's herd, the same one Evie rode every time she stopped by the Friessen family ranch. They were high in the hills, the sun was bright, and the day was warm.

Danny didn't say anything, only glanced her way, wearing that ratty cowboy hat, one she'd swear he'd grown into. His arms were tanned in his faded red shirt.

"You were having a good time with Rand last night. You had fun?" he asked.

What could she say? She wasn't about to mope around. "Well, yeah. Dinner out, great company… I wasn't about to focus on problems I can't do anything about. Is that what this is about, or is it more about the fight you were having with Charlie?"

She'd noticed the tension. Charlie had gone from hanging off Danny, stealing a kiss, to being quiet. Evie had seen Danny mad before, and he wasn't the type of guy anyone could push around. Whatever Charlie said had thrown the entire evening off between the two of them. Charlie had finally given up on talking to him as he finished his beer.

He glanced her way again but then walked on, leading them. That was something he'd always done. He wasn't the kind of guy who followed along with anything. Evie thought back to the night before. Rand had been kind of fun, but she'd picked up on the fact that he was all talk and kind of handsy. She was glad Danny had driven her home, allowing her to avoid the obligatory kiss.

"You know, Danny, you're not the easiest guy to be around when you're in a mood. I guess I could continue to do all the talking and come to my own conclusions about what's up between you and Charlie. Obviously, she said something that pushed every one of your buttons."

It wasn't lost on her that she was there alone with Danny on this ride. There was no Charlie now.

He still said nothing and then pulled his horse to a stop, resting his arm on the saddle horn. "I don't like being directed, pushed, or to feel like I'm being manipulated," he said matter of factly and cryptically. Now she couldn't help wondering what Charlie had said. As she'd sat alone in the back seat the night before, she hadn't missed that Danny was brooding over something.

Charlie had carried the entire conversation all the way back to her place.

"You want me to comment on that, or are you just stating an obvious fact?" she said and took in the look Danny gave her. "Just saying, no one likes being manipulated. I take it you and Charlie are…what?" Dating, sleeping together, taking a break? She didn't have a clue. She wanted to know, was dying to know, but she and Danny didn't share that kind of personal stuff.

He glanced up to the sky and seemed to be lost in thought, then directed his megawatt blue eyes at her, giving her all of his attention. He'd suddenly turned serious. "You showed up here last weekend, and I thought something was off, wrong. Then yesterday I dropped by the restaurant because when I called your cell phone, it had been disconnected."

The giant lump inside her stomach that had been a powerful ache over the past few weeks was only getting worse as she felt herself slipping deeper into a dark hole. "So you don't want to talk about Charlie, but you want to talk about the fact that something had to give with me? I had a choice to make." She shrugged as she glanced off in the distance, taking in the view. It was beautiful, and just being out there, it was as if she could shake off all her troubles and leave them behind for an hour or two. It was a freedom she needed right now, and Danny was refusing to give her that. "I don't have the cash to pay it. Dad's restaurant is barely making anything. I'm helping as best I can, but I haven't been paid anything in…" *A month*, she thought, but she couldn't share that. She'd told her dad she was fine and didn't need it. He had so many bills and was struggling to pay suppliers and stay afloat. Even though her bank account was so low she didn't even have the twenty-dollar minimum left to withdraw, it wasn't that bad.

"So that's why you were bringing up other jobs. You know, Evie, if you need something…" He stopped, and maybe he knew not to say any more from the horror on her face. Before he could start again, she kicked up the mare into a trot, moving around Danny to the open field.

"Evie, wait!" he called out, spurring his horse to a canter to catch up to her. "I didn't mean to put you on the spot. I'm just saying I can loan you money until you figure out something else—or let me help you find something else!" Then he reached for her reins to pull her horse to a stop.

She couldn't remember ever being so angry, so she jumped off and started walking, digging into each step, hearing him swear behind her. She glanced back to see he'd abandoned both horses and was now coming after her. She didn't know why, but she started running.

He was on her, his arms around her waist, lifting her, pulling her against him and all his hardness, which had her wanting to lean into him, but feeling that only made her angry, so she fought his arms, pounding at him.

"Let me go, Danny!" she yelled and kicked her legs in the air, but damn, he was strong.

"Stop it, Evie! Seriously, I'm just trying to help."

He set her down, and she whipped around, breathing hard, still feeling his hands around her. She was angry at how he was making her feel, so she shoved him with both her hands, but he was like a damn rock. She did it again, and this time he grabbed her arms, and she fought with everything she had against him. Then she was in his arms, and he was kissing her, and she was kissing him back, wanting him closer, tasting him as if she couldn't get enough of him.

Her hands were twisted in his shirt, and his hands were yanking at hers, pulling it free from her jeans as he held her close to him. The roughness, the depth of the kiss, she needed to have more. Then she was on the ground on the grass, and he was on top of her, pressing into her as her legs wrapped around him.

He stopped, and he just took in her face. Then he was standing, and she didn't miss the bulge in his jeans, the size of him. It was almost embarrassing that she wanted him so much. At the same time, he turned to the side as if trying to pull himself together. "I'm sorry," he said. "I shouldn't have done that." He didn't look at her, and all she wanted to do was shut her eyes and curl up somewhere and hide.

"Takes two, Danny. I shouldn't have hit you." She was shaking inside from want, need. She didn't know it, but she'd never dared to think of her and Danny as anything but friends.

He held out his hand, and she grasped it, letting him pull her up, but she kept her distance, and so did he, even though she wanted nothing more than to throw herself at him. She stared at the ground and fought like all hell to pull herself back together.

"You're stubborn," he added, and she took in the mischief that stared back at her.

"Look who's calling who what. Take a long look in the mirror, cowboy. Pretty sure you invented the term."

He nodded and glanced away. What was he thinking? She'd give anything to know, but they were in uncharted territory. Was that kiss something he'd wanted? She wanted to ask, needed to know.

"I just need to say one thing," he said. "If you need anything, any money, help, anything, I want you to promise me you'll let me help."

There it was, the spell broken. She had no intention of sharing any of her pathetic life, nor the fact that she was so broke that if something didn't change, that last twenty dollars that had just gone into her gas tank would have her walking in a matter of days.

She patted his chest as she walked past him. "Let's go for a ride," she said, and as she glanced back after mounting the mare that had been happily grazing, she sensed a distance with Danny that hadn't been there before.

Chapter Eight

Danny and Evie had the quietest ride back to the ranch. For the first time in his life, he'd followed behind her, seeing how she sat in the saddle, stiff and straight—seeing her as a woman. Why had he never seen her this way? He must have, on some level, he realized as he remembered kissing her as he had, taking her to the ground, where he'd had to fight against his intense desire to strip her naked and bury himself in her in the tall grass, where he could taste every inch of her, his friend, whom he'd known since they were kids. How he'd been able to pull back, he'd never know, and he was embarrassed still at how he'd behaved, like a caveman. She had every right to be furious with him. It wasn't lost on him how she'd responded to each kiss, though, as he'd tasted her deeply. She'd pulled him closer and yanked at his shirt as if she couldn't get close enough.

After unsaddling the horses and brushing them down, he noted her unwillingness to burden him with her problems, but then, he wasn't about to share what he was feeling about Charlie, either. Charlie was sexy and hot and fun, but she didn't drive him to the madness he was feeling now.

"Later, Danny," Evie called out, the first thing she'd said since that kiss. She was walking toward her truck, and the door squealed as she opened it and climbed in.

He was already moving her way and was at her truck when she closed the door, his hand on the open window. She was looking straight ahead, not at him, and he didn't know how to break the tension that rippled between them.

"We should talk about what happened," he said, not that he wanted to. He was about as good at sharing as she was, which meant their communication totally sucked.

She looked his way and leaned back in the bench seat. "About what, exactly?"

Was she kidding? He leveled a heavy gaze her way and noticed her blush, not something he'd ever seen her do. "About what happened up in that field. I kissed you, you kissed me."

She squeezed her eyes shut and covered her face. He didn't reach out to touch her even though that was all he wanted to do. "We're seriously going to have this conversation? I thought you'd ignore it and let me just drive away with at least my dignity intact—or partially." She still wasn't looking his way, and he didn't have a clue what she was thinking. Maybe she regretted the whole thing.

"Evie, look at me. We've been friends for too long to let this happen. What kind of guy do you think I am?"

She slapped the steering wheel, and he took in the flash in her eyes, the fire spitting his way. "I don't know, Danny. Maybe not even twenty-four hours ago, you were kissing another girl, and you seemed to love having her hanging off your arm, but then you had some disagreement and all of a sudden you're grabbing me and kissing me?"

She stopped talking, and he had to step back, because it was like a slap in the face. She was right. He wasn't being fair to anyone. She started her truck and gave it gas as it sputtered and threatened to stall, the engine loud, the muffler shot.

"Evie, wait…"

"No, Danny, stop." She cut him off. "This is too much, and the only thing I want to do is go home. Let me leave at least with some dignity. I'm not the girl you can play with and have fun with and kiss and screw and then walk away. We're not strangers. We've known each other forever, and you're, what, dating someone else? I'm not made to be okay with that and then for us to remain friends. You know whoever came up with the term 'friends with benefits' wasn't talking about us!"

She shoved her truck in reverse, backing up, and he let her go. He watched her drive away, noting her burnt-out tail light. He wanted to get in his Bronco and go after her, pull her over and fix it for her, but it wouldn't be welcome, not right now.

"Something going on here?"

He turned to see his dad walking his way, and his mom, too, both dressed in faded jeans and T-shirts. It looked as if they were about to saddle some horses and go for a ride. He could tell by their expressions they'd likely heard everything.

"Evie seemed kind of upset," his mom added, and his dad was staring at him with a look that said yup, they'd heard it all.

"It's fine," he said, but his parents were both staring at the dust in the distance from Evie's truck.

"Someone needs to tell Evie her tail light is burned out," Diana said. "That's a ticket she's not going to want to get."

"Not sure that truck is even safe to be on the road anymore, Danny," His dad added.

"I was going to go after her just now..." he started and took in the intensity staring back at him from his parents. They were patient, and his dad wasn't one to add his two cents often, but he couldn't figure out why his mom wasn't all over this, especially after hearing what Evie had said.

"You know, Danny, we've raised you well," His dad said. "You clear on your feelings for Charlie and Evie? You've been close friends with Evie, growing up together, and you're, what, confused all of a sudden about your feelings and how she fits?" He tossed an uneasy look to Diana, who was still staring in the distance where Evie had gone. She didn't say anything.

"Charlie and I aren't serious," he said. Boy, that was lame, and he shut his eyes for a second, giving his head a shake, resting his hands on his hips. He couldn't help feeling embarrassed. If he wasn't clear on his feelings, then Evie was right.

"So you kissed Evie, who is probably close to down and out, from what you said the other night, and what, Danny?" his mom said. "You want her to have fun and fool around with you? That's like saying you have no respect for her. Seriously, don't you know that Evie has had feelings for you for like forever?"

Danny could see how bothered she was, but he also knew she was wrong. "Mom, Evie is my buddy. She doesn't have feelings like that. I would've known." His cell phone beeped, and he reached in his pocket to pull it out. It was a text from Charlie: *Can we talk?* He pocketed his phone.

Maybe his parents knew, as his mom was now giving him that look she had when he'd done something wrong as a child. His dad said nothing.

"Danny, you need to get real clear on what you want," Diana said. "Toying around with two girls, one of them a close friend you supposedly care about, isn't the way to handle things. You need to sit down with Evie and talk to her. You owe her that. You've been friends for too long to toss away that relationship. There are some lines you don't cross unless you're clear on your intentions. I know you're not thoughtless, but one sure-fire way to hurt her is to do exactly what you've done."

Now he really felt like crap. His cell phone beeped again, and he knew it was likely Charlie. If anything, she was persistent. He ignored it. "Okay, fine, I'll talk to her," he snapped and took in his parents' faces.

His dad was shaking his head. "Yeah, you should, but only after you figure out what you want. Is this thing with Charlie serious?" His dad asked.

Danny took in the way his mom was staring at him. He knew she didn't really care for Charlie. His dad…he didn't know what to think. He shrugged, and his mom just lifted her hands.

"Maybe you should have a word with your son," she said, then walked away back to the house.

"What's that about?" Danny said.

"Oh, you know, this thing with you and Charlie. I think your mom has secretly had this hope that you and Evie would find your way together one day. I guess you need to figure out who it is you want." His dad rubbed his head. "Some of the things you said about Charlie yesterday and her letting things slip about Evie's dad left us both kind of unsettled. To have your privacy invaded like that… If Charlie's dad is talking to her about one client's business, who else is he talking about? It can't be isolated, and I'm not comfortable keeping any business in a place where someone has loose lips. Charlie may be a looker, flashy and fun, but is that the kind of girl you want to have a life with?"

Was his dad kidding? He was just starting his life. He had law school to look forward to and had no intention of settling down right now with a wife. No! He was single and planned to stay that way. Marriage was something for after he finished law school and the grueling hours. He hadn't planned anything that far ahead.

"Dad, I'm like twenty-one. I'm not getting married. I'm just having fun, nothing serious," he said again, wondering why he was feeling as if everyone needed him to decide on something.

"I never said you had to get married tomorrow, and I hope you don't, but at the same time, girls like Charlie are made for certain people. I just don't think you're one of them. Your uncle Brad made that mistake once, settling on flash and looks and not much else, and she was walking trouble, too—not that I know Charlie! But blowing in here in a fancy car a kid her age has no business driving, an overpriced sports car that her father bought her, that she didn't earn… You get serious with a girl like that, she comes with certain expectations." His dad was shaking his head and rested his hand on his shoulder. "And Evie, well, you already know what we think of her. You know that girl well, so maybe you should think about what you're doing and how Evie falls into all of that."

Then his dad was walking away back to the house, and his phone dinged again. He pulled it out, seeing new texts.

I'm sorry was the last one from Charlie, and before that, *Please call me.*

Chapter Nine

What was he doing? Listening to Charlie apologize for how she'd acted the night before made him feel like crap because of how he was feeling toward not just her but also Evie, his good friend. He'd crossed a line, and there was something to be said about time and the ability to look back on what he'd done.

Charlie was like a drug, and she made him feel good. She was the type he was drawn to, the heat, the sex, just wanting to feel all her softness, and she wanted him. She had more depth than he'd originally thought, including compassion. That was something he'd not expected.

Then there was Evie, and he could barely stand to think about how he'd grabbed her and pawed at her. She'd touched him in a way he'd never experienced before. He understood her on a level he'd never understood anyone else, and coming from a place where they were good friends, they could talk about anything and had shared just about everything. She was the one person he could count on to always be in his corner. She was the polar opposite of Charlie, and the thought of hurting her was absolutely killing him.

He saw the car pull in, the red Mustang, from where he was upstairs in his loft, rinsing out a bowl after having just downed cereal for dinner. She was as stylish as ever in jeans and a simple short T-shirt that showed her amazing bust even from his window. She was looking around, a woman who didn't take no for an answer—but then, he hadn't responded to her texts with a call or anything.

"Hello, Danny?"

He could hear her footsteps on the concrete of the barn. "Up here," he called out, looking over the railing and seeing her looking up at him. Her long dark hair was brushed straight. She gave him a tight smile.

"You're ignoring me," she said, standing there, looking up at him, and then she started up the wooden steps as if she had every right.

He said nothing, because the fact was that he didn't know what to say, and seeing her now, walking up the stairs, the attraction was still there. What was wrong with him? Her hand was on the railing as she stepped into the loft, taking in the space: his unmade bed, a sofa and a flat screen in the corner, and his small kitchenette. What was she thinking? She wasn't the kind of girl he could see fitting into a place like this.

"You know, you live up to your nickname well. I can understand now why everyone calls you Mr. Mysterious. The way you're looking at me and saying nothing, it could give a girl a complex or crush all my remaining self-esteem. Say something, please. Did you get my texts?"

Danny glanced to the side, over to the small round

table where his cell phone was sitting. "I did," he said, and he wanted to add, *Sorry I didn't get back to you, sorry I'm such an asshole, and sorry I kissed Evie and I don't know what to say to either of you.* He could see how she was on edge even though she hid it well.

"You're still mad, I can tell," she said. "I'm sorry I pushed, Danny. It's one of my flaws when I care about someone, and I have such strong feelings for you. I think I'm in love with you, or falling hard for you, and I want only the best for you. Mentioning you as I did to my dad and his friend, Hank Billows, talking about you, your drive, your compassion, the focus you have to be the best you can be, well…"

Danny was stuck on the falling in love part and the name Hank Billows. He knew it well. Who didn't in the legal world? He was one of those top names, like Alan Dershowitz or Barry Scheck. He realized Charlie was still talking. "You're telling me your dad's friend is *the* Hank Billows?" he said, interrupting. He didn't want to talk about her feelings for him, as that only added to his discomfort. She was moving way too fast, which reminded him of what his dad had said earlier.

Charlie paused, and then a smile touched her lips as she walked closer. "Yes, the very same. Now do you see why I was pushing so hard? For him to take interest in you says a lot, but I promise I won't mention it again, and I won't push the fact that he still has so many connections back in Chicago that one phone call would have you working there this summer. I won't mention it again. You just continue on with doing things your way."

He said nothing, thinking of the cases Hank had argued. He'd set precedents that were still being studied.

He was a top mind in the field and a man Danny seriously wouldn't have minded sitting down to talk with. Then there was Charlie here, now. He could reach out right now and touch her, she was so close, but he kept his hands where they were, one on the rail, the other on his hip.

She reached over and touched his chest, the flat of his stomach, and her eyes drifted up to him. She pulled her lower lip between her teeth. What was she doing, offering herself up to him? Her hands were like a slice of heaven, so he gripped her wrist and pulled it off him, shaking his head.

"Don't you want me?" she said as he walked away, stepping around the table, needing to clear his head and block out the sexual energy that was ramping up in his loft. With his bed right there, he knew he could strip her down in a second and bury himself inside her to ease some of his discomfort, which only added to his guilt. What was it about Charlie that had him considering doing just that?

He pressed his hands on the chair back and took her in. "That's the problem, Charlie. I do want you, but I'm not clear on how I feel about you."

She started over to him, and he squeezed the back of the chair again harder until she was standing right in front of him, looking at him with confusion and wanting. He was seeing what it could be with her.

"Wanting me is good. Why are you overthinking everything?" she said, and she rested her hand on his arm so carefully and stared as she ran it up over his triceps, biceps, to his shoulder, allowing her eyes to linger and then lock on to his.

He had to look away, because she was doing it again.

Just being with her was confusing the hell out of him. Maybe he just needed sex. It had been a long time, but seeing how Charlie was hooking into him was bringing him a seesaw of confusion. Did he want her? Then there was Evie.

Charlie's hand was still pressed to his arm, running up and down and then tracing circles. She was so deliberate, and he turned, facing her as her hand pressed over his stomach again and then down to his belt buckle, skimming over it and lower. He hissed as she touched him, and he grabbed her wrist again, holding her away even though he wanted to weep from the loss of her touch.

"You should know that I don't know how I feel about you. We aren't really anything, Charlie. Going out a few times… You should know I kissed Evie yesterday, and I feel like absolute crap."

There it was, shock, what he needed to cool his desire. She was holding her hand and then fisting it, and he couldn't tell whether she was getting ready to slug him or walk away. She should walk away, but was that what he wanted?

She pulled her arms around herself and slowly looked up to him. "Are you in love with her?" she asked.

Danny walked away, back over to the railing, leaning down and staring at the empty stairwell. "Evie and I are friends. We have been since we were kids. Of course I love her that way, but more than that, I don't know, just like I don't really know how I feel about you," he said as he heard her cross over to him and lean down on the rail beside him. This time, she didn't try to touch him, and he wasn't sure what was going through her head.

"So I still have a chance with you, then," she said. It

was the one thing he hadn't expected her to say. He said nothing, and she tossed him an easy hesitant smile and nudged him with her shoulder. "Just give us a chance, give me a chance."

He just took her in, her image, her narrow nose, her full lips, the shape of her brows, and the light makeup she wore, which made her eyes really pop, eyes that were filled with so much passion and light and fun.

"Don't say anything." She rested her hand over his mouth. "Just come for dinner tomorrow night, no pretense, no… Just come for dinner, meet my family." She pulled her hand away and then pressed a kiss to his lips, so gentle. Then she pulled back and headed for the steps.

Instead of being clear and knowing what he wanted, he was even more confused.

"Six, come by," she said. "I'll see you then."

"Just dinner," he said. "Charlie, no promises for us, and this doesn't mean we're together."

Her wide smile was far more confident now. "I know, but it's something. Just give yourself a chance, and me. I think you'll see that you won't be able to resist me. But, Danny, you need to get clear on Evie too."

Then she was gone down the steps, and he listened to her footsteps on concrete as she walked out of the barn. He knew he owed it to both Charlie and Evie to get his head screwed on straight.

Chapter Ten

E vie had hitched a ride to work with her dad. Opening for lunch on a Sunday was something he'd never done before, but he was now hoping to cash in on the weekend business. Evie needed to figure out something else to do. It wasn't that she hadn't been putting some serious thought into her future, because that was all she'd done as of late. She had a high school diploma, and she was living with her parents, working for her dad, trying to keep his dream of the barbecue restaurant alive, but the reality was that the restaurant industry had the lowest success rate. More eateries died a painful, slow death than succeeded, and even her parents, as they'd sat at the kitchen table that morning, had come to the conclusion that something had to give.

Her dad could always start butchering again at the superstore, and her mom was picking up shifts again at the drycleaners. Evie needed to polish up a resume and start knocking on doors. There were always the local fast food joints, which seemed to have openings. It would be a minimum-wage job that would at least get gas in her truck, which was now sitting at home, empty. Or she could suck it up and walk next door to the chain restaurant, which was always busy, and pick up a job serving tables, hoping for more from tips.

She heard the ding above the door and turned to see Danny, dressed in blue jeans and a light blue western shirt with snaps and a heavy buckle. His deep red hair and blue eyes nearly had her knees giving out on her, and she took in his amazing build, remembering what it felt like to have him pressed against her, wanting her. She had to fight the warmth that filled her and could feel her cheeks start to burn again. She'd never in her life been uncomfortable around Danny, and now, seeing him walking toward her, she had to fight the urge to hide.

"Hi, was wondering if we could talk," he said. The intensity with which he was staring at her had her fisting her hands on the counter to try to gather her footing again.

She wanted to say, *Sorry, we're busy working here,* but not a customer had come in yet. Her dad was in back and would be able to hear everything, too, and that she couldn't have.

"Dad, I'm going to take a break," she called out, and she heard him yell back to go ahead. She walked around the counter and over to the corner by the window, where she pulled out a stool and sat. It was far enough away that her dad wouldn't be able to hear. Danny pulled out the stool opposite her and straddled it. It wasn't lost on her how much bigger he was in comparison to her petiteness. He smiled, and it was awkward.

"Okay, so talk," she said. She could've made this easier, but she was a frickin' mess, with how she was feeling after the day before. She'd barely slept, tossing and turning in the night and waking in a sweat at the image of her and Danny together naked in bed, skin to skin, feeling him inside her and on her. It was horrible, because she'd never allowed herself to think of him this way, and now this was the only way she could think of him.

He rested his hands on the round tabletop. He was so close she could touch him, but instead she was seeing those hands and imagining what they would be like running over her naked skin. "I'm sorry for what I did, for how I behaved."

Her heart sank a little more. "For…" she prompted him, because it hurt to not be wanted.

"The way I reacted with you, chasing you down and kissing you and almost…" He stopped, and she could see the difficulty he was having saying it. Yes, he'd wanted her, but he was a guy, and guys were about sex. She'd just never expected that from Danny. It was a loss that she realized would likely haunt her forever.

"Well, I realize I'm not a stacked supermodel who's all that experienced with guys, but I didn't think kissing me could be that bad," she said. She couldn't figure out why her smart mouth always went to sarcasm. She thought he'd laugh, but instead his expression seemed angry.

"You don't get it, Evie. That's not what I'm saying. I care about you so damn much that I didn't think, and then I was kissing you, and the problem was I was so close to ripping your clothes off and burying myself in you, riding you in that grass like an animal, and I didn't want to stop, because I never expected to want to kiss you as I did."

Whoa! She hadn't expected that reaction, not from Danny. She didn't have a clue what to say, as her mouth gaped and nothing but a squeak came out.

He sat up straighter, looking around at the emptiness of the place and back to Evie. "You're my friend, and just the thought of tossing that friendship away because I can't get clear on what this is? Then there's Charlie," he said, and that had her pulling back, sitting straighter, her hands fisted in her lap.

"So let me get this straight," she said. "You think you have feelings for me, but then you also have feelings for Charlie, and you need to, what, take a step back, evaluate, figure out where I fit in? Or is it that you want to choose who you want in your life, and you want me and Charlie to just sit back and wait?" She gestured at him and took in the confusion on his face.

"That's not what I mean," he said. "What I'm trying to say is how important you are to me, and I'm bothered by the line I crossed, taking our relationship to something I never intended. I don't know what's wrong with me or why I did it or why it is I can't forget that kiss, or you, and the feelings I'm now feeling for you aren't those of a friend."

She sat straighter, hearing what he was saying and feeling sick, because it was as if he was deciding who he wanted more, and she couldn't be that girl. She couldn't be the kind of girl who waited on the sidelines to see if she would be picked. She'd done that all her life in just about everything else, and it didn't feel good, not at all.

"I see," she said, swallowing the giant ache that was building in her chest and in her throat, threatening to erupt into something that could have her curled up in a corner, crying. Not that she was one of those girls, but everyone had a breaking point, and she realized Danny was hers. This here, this moment, could break her. Nothing in her life was going her way, and everything was such a damn struggle right now. "So you're asking for what from me, exactly, Danny?" She pulled a breath, long and deep. Her hands were shaking, and she tucked them between her thighs as she sat straight, feeling the strain in her shoulders.

"I'm asking you to forgive me. I have school to finish, and then I'm off to law school next year, and I need to know that we're okay, that we're still friends, that…"

She tilted her head, sensing the "but," or maybe he was trying to get her to agree to forget what had happened and pretend she didn't know what it was like to have his lips on her, his tongue tasting her, his large hands rough and running over her, feeling her intimate curves, to feel his desire pressed against her. If he said it, it would crush her, because she never believed Danny to be that shallow. She could make it easier, or not.

"I don't want to lose you in my life, and I just need some time to figure out me and what I want."

"You mean who you want," she added, and before he could say anything else, she slid off the stool and stood, keeping the table between them, taking in the way he wiped his face, the way he seemed on edge, returning to the quiet deep thinker she'd known him as. She rested her hand on the table, staring at the dings and scratches and tiny chunks taken out of the wood.

"I'll make it easy for you." She stared at her hand, refusing to look up at him. "I'm not interested in being a choice for you, the girl who'll maybe be waiting for you, so you just go on with Charlie, and I'll…" She stopped and then flicked her gaze up, taking in his shock, not sure whether he was relieved or hurt. "I'll see you around," she said.

Then she walked away back to the counter, pausing only once to see Danny slipping off the stool and standing there, watching her. Before he could say another word, she slipped through the doors to the back room, past her dad, who looked up from where he was butchering ribs, and she took off out the back, where Danny couldn't find her.

Chapter Eleven

He pulled in the round circular driveway up to the impressive two-story home that was a mix of brick and frame, surrounded by bushes filled with different flowers.

Charlie's bright red Mustang was parked with the top up and windows rolled up in front of an open triple-car garage. Parked inside were a Mercedes, a white Cadillac, and what looked like one of the newer model Humvees. He stepped out of his Bronco, seeing how it looked so out of place as he passed a silver BMW and started up the circular wide front steps.

The door popped open, and the joy that shone from Charlie's face should have warmed him. She was wearing a long slimming skirt, black heels, and a loose cream tank over what he thought was a black bra, based on the straps showing. Her arms linked around his neck, and she pressed her incredible body against him. All he could think about was the hurt he'd seen in Evie's face and the loss he couldn't shake of something greater, Evie's friendship.

He wondered whether there was a special place in hell reserved for him after what he'd done. If he could just go back… That had been all he could think of as he drove to Charlie's, wishing he'd cancelled. But he'd caused enough hurt that day. He wasn't going to add to that.

"What's wrong?" Charlie asked, and he took in how she looked at him with such intensity. Yeah, she really did care for him. That was a given. He could see it, and it only caused his heart to ache more because he didn't feel the same. He just shook his head, not trusting his mouth to make anything better.

"Not sure I'm the greatest company right now," he said, but Charlie just steered him, linking her arm through his, leading him inside.

"Don't be silly. You're here, and that's all that counts. Besides, don't dismiss my charm and ability to cheer you up," she teased, holding him as she led him inside. The entrance was huge, and he looked up to the high ceiling as they walked past an impressively decorated living room, a massive kitchen that was five times the size of his parents', and a second family room with tons of windows. In the back yard, two men were sitting at a patio table. The umbrella was up. Danny recognized her dad. The other man had gray hair, and he couldn't see his face.

"Mom, this is Danny," Charlie said. "Danny, this is my mom, Sandra."

He'd never seen the woman in the kitchen. Her dark hair didn't show a speck of gray, and she was tall and fit, in a sleeveless shirt that showed she worked out.

"Danny Friessen, I've heard nothing but great things

about you," she said. Now he knew where Charlie got her smile from. She was tearing up lettuce at a center island. "I can see my daughter wasn't kidding when she went on and on about how handsome you are. So glad you can join us for dinner, and hope we see lots more of you."

"Great to meet you, Missus—"

"Sandra, please," she said, cutting him off. "Never liked that mister and missus stuff, always made me cringe. Mrs. Adams is Perry's mom, and I found myself looking over my shoulder when someone would call me that, wondering if she was standing there." At the face she made, he wanted to laugh. She was warm and welcoming, and he hadn't expected that. "You go on out there with the men. Charlie, why don't you get your young man a drink?"

Then Danny was outside on the patio, and Perry was standing, his hand out, as Charlie introduced them.

"Hey, so glad you could come join us, Danny," Perry said. "This is a friend of mine, Hank Billows. Him and I go way back."

Danny looked down at the lawyer who was a legend. He was distinguished, with white hair, distinct features, and blue eyes that were almost gray. He didn't stand up. He, like Charlie's father, was wearing golf attire, one in light, the other in shades of blue, ultra conservative. Danny pulled a chair out, and Charlie rested her hand on his shoulder as he sat.

"You want a beer, Danny?" she asked.

He took in the cocktails both Perry and Hank had in front of them. He could smell the bourbon, or he thought so, anyway. "Sure," he said, and then Charlie was gone back into the house, leaving him with the men, taking in the landscaping of the huge yard, the pool, the decks, and the grass, all well manicured.

"So Charlie was mentioning that you're studying to become a lawyer," Perry said as he leaned back in the mesh chair. He was in the shade, and Danny could feel the sun beating down on him. He wondered too, dressed as he was, in a blue western shirt and his nicer blue jeans, if he shouldn't have dressed up a bit more.

"I am, but then, my mom's a lawyer, too."

"I was telling you about her, Hank," Perry said. "Diana Friessen, small-time stuff here, mostly wills, estates, litigation. How many years has your mom been practicing in these parts now?"

Danny wasn't sure how comfortable he was talking about his mom and her business. "A few years now. She put us kids first and waited until Mark was in school to start practicing again."

Hank was holding a glass, taking a swallow. His gaze never wavered from Danny. Then Charlie appeared with a bottle of beer, not the kind Danny drank but rather an import, and a glass of white wine, obviously for her.

"Thank you," he said as Charlie took the seat beside him and gave him a bold smile. He twisted off the cap and ignored the glass she'd also put there for him, instead lifting the bottle to his lips.

"So what are your plans after law school, Danny?" Hank finally asked.

He'd kind of expected that, but he'd not put a whole lot of thought into it. He was expecting to settle back in the area, helping out folks who needed so much more.

"Pass the bar and come back here, settle in the area. My family's here," he added, but he also knew that wasn't what he'd really meant. Everyone else focused on ambitious things, articling under some Supreme Court justice, interning in a top firm, working under the best of the best, climbing the corporate ladder.

"Charlie was mentioning that you're at the top of your class. Any chances you're thinking of maybe trying out one of the big law firms out east? You can learn a lot out there, trying cases you'd never see here. Getting your feet wet in that arena can open a lot of doors anywhere for you," Hank added.

Danny didn't say anything as he slid his glance to the side, taking in Charlie, who was taking a sip of her wine. This was supposed to have been just dinner.

"Oh, I'm still working on Danny," she said, "hoping to convince him to give Chicago a try."

He couldn't get over this thing she seemed to have with Chicago. Her dad laughed, holding his glass up.

"Danny, one thing you'll learn soon enough about my daughter, and her mother is the same, is that once she's set her mind on something, there's little chance you have of changing it. My advice is that it's best to just align yourself with whatever it is she's thinking and get good and comfortable with it. You know, happy wife, happy life. My girl has had her heart set on moving to Chicago since visiting Hank there before he hung up his shingle. When you get a bug for a place, it kind of sticks with you. You ever been to Chicago, Danny?"

What could he say? He wasn't interested. "No, never been out east. Would be nice to visit, I suppose," he said —sometime down the road, that was, when he wasn't cramming for tests and studying but was established with a law degree and a life. Then he'd travel and see some places with his wife and kids. He fidgeted in his chair over that thought, because that picture was down the road, and the face of his wife wasn't clear. He glanced over to Charlie, who leaned his way and smiled.

"You should give it a chance," Hank said. "It's not for everyone, but before you make your decision on where you want to be and settle and practice, you should check out all your options. Opportunities are vast in bigger places. I think Charlie here is planning on August out there, am I right?" He gestured to her where she sat comfortably beside Danny.

"We'll see. I guess plans change." She was looking right at Danny. "Sometimes you meet a person who becomes more important than a place you've always wanted to go."

Danny didn't know what to say, how to respond to that, because he'd never expected Charlie to be the kind of girl who would consider changing her life and wants for him. Instead of warming his heart or making him feel as if she was the one, it had him questioning everything about what he wanted and feeling worse than he was now, leading Charlie on in some way, giving her a false hope that there could be something everlasting with him.

"Charlie, can you give me a hand putting everything out on the table?" Her mom appeared in the door, and Charlie excused herself and went inside.

Danny took in her father and Hank watching him, their expressions questioning.

"You know, Danny," Perry set his glass on the table, "my daughter has never had the kind of feelings for a young man that she has for you. I sincerely hope you're not toying with her and that this thing between the two of you makes her happy. If my daughter is happy, then I'm happy. For her to say she's willing to give up moving to a place she's dreamed of going for as long as I can remember, well, that gives me pause and leads me to ask you what you're willing to give up for my daughter."

Danny squeezed the bottle of beer, feeling the scrutiny of a father. If he were wearing a collar, he'd likely be pulling at it, as he felt the dampness soaking through his shirt at his underarms. "Charlie and I have only started dating. We're getting to know each other. I care for her, but there's no more than that," he stated.

The two men exchanged a glance. Hank Billows excused himself and left.

"I can see that," Perry said, "but my daughter is already seeing a future with you. So if you're not comfortable with that or she's just a phase for you and you'll be moving on…"

Whoa! Geez, two dates in and everyone was thinking they were heading down the aisle to marriage. "You know what, Mr. Adams? I can understand you wanting to make sure your daughter doesn't get hurt, and I'm not the kind of guy who would treat her with any disrespect or disregard her feelings, but I think everyone needs to dial it back a bit. We've only dated a few times, and we're just getting to know each other, so…" He took in the smile on Perry Adams' face before he lifted his glass and downed the rest of the bourbon.

"Point taken, son, and glad to hear you have some values—but let me also give you some advice. Women will already have the wedding planned before you even get around to that line of thinking." He raised his brows just as Charlie and her mom appeared with plates and a dinner of chicken and cut potatoes.

Danny was stuck on the need to pull Charlie aside before he left and have a sit down about where things were, exactly, with them.

Chapter Twelve

It was Monday morning, and her dad and mom were both gone. Evie powered up the desktop to polish up what she could of her resume. She heard a car and went to the door, seeing the familiar black pickup. Danny's mom stepped out, her vibrant red hair hanging in waves. She wore a blue and white shirt over a plain skirt that went to her knees.

"Evie, hope you don't mind me dropping by like this," Diana said. She was so warm, and Evie had known her forever. She'd had her cuts and scrapes patched up by her, and she still had a fondness for her.

"No, not at all, come on in. Sorry for the…" Disarray, mess, unkemptness? There had been a lack of everything, time, focus, and money, as of late.

Diana just swept her hand as if it were no big deal. "I came to see you. Don't worry so much. How are you doing, anyways?"

Evie heard the door close as Diana stepped in. The light spilled into the living room. The dark brown sofa was covered with a flowered blanket to hide a stain, the shag carpet was from the seventies, and the paneling was light oak and had been there since she could remember. "I'm good, you know. Do you want some tea?" She wandered into the kitchen, hoping to all hell they had tea. She knew there was only half a tin of coffee left.

"No, no, don't trouble yourself. Listen, I wanted to stop in and have a talk with you. You know we've known each other for how long, sixteen, seventeen years? Danny and you have been friends all that time." Diana took a seat at the kitchen table. It was clean and wiped down, but then, the house was just old and dated, not untidy.

Evie took the seat across from Diana, seeing something there in her expression, and for a moment she didn't want her to say anything. "Did Danny talk to you?" she said. She was mortified, thinking Diana was there on Danny's behalf.

"Well, he talked with me about helping you out with a job. We've known for a while your dad has been struggling to keep that restaurant afloat, but it's just the industry. It's a great place, great food, but sometimes it's just not enough. Economics, location, and marketing, it's all tied together, and you've stuck around to help out your folks, which is admirable, but…"

Did everyone know how dire a spot her parents were in, she was in? "Look, I'm looking for a job, so it's nothing to worry about. I'll pick up something. It's just life, you know."

Diana shrugged. "Hey, I get it better than anyone, Evie. You have a great family, I like your mom and dad, and you're right: Hard times hit everyone at some point in their life and in some way. I'm here to help, to do something. I mean I'd like to hire you. Come and work for me. You have…"

Evie just stared at Diana, feeling like crap because this seemed like pity. "So is this from Danny?" she asked, and Diana gave her a hard look.

"No, this is from me. I know the kind of girl you are, Evie, and I do need help. My case load is getting so heavy…"

Evie started shaking her head. "I'm not sure what you think I can do, but I can tell you that for paper and legal stuff, you should probably look at one of the academic types. I can't type for the life of me, I'm a two-finger girl on the keyboard, and my people skills are—"

"Are you kidding me? Your skills with everyone are what set you apart," Diana said.

Evie wondered, as she took in Danny's mom, whether she was kidding.

Diana laughed. "Your face right now, the way you're looking at me, I want that. You say it like it is, girl, and I like that. Besides, you won't be pushing paper, per se—some, yes, but I need some help staying organized, and Jed and I also need someone to help out with the riding school. There's a lot to do to stay on top of things, and we keep talking about hiring someone full time, but we never do. We've been dividing it up between Danny and Christopher and Mark helping out, which is almost painful, and Jed is about the worst for organizing. It doesn't take someone with a degree. It's going to take someone who knows us, who can fit in."

Evie crossed her arms, feeling a light being held out to her as if she could breathe easy for a minute, but then it hit her: This would mean seeing Danny. Ugh, that darkness and ache in her gut came back even stronger.

She felt her shoulders pull and sag as she leaned in more. "You know what? I would love nothing more than to give it a try even though I know Danny put you up to it, but being there…" She had to clear her throat, taking in the way Diana was staring at her, leaning on the table, waiting her out. "I don't think it would be the best idea, considering where Danny and I are right now, for me to be around."

To see him with Charlie… No, maybe it was best that she looked at other options that wouldn't have her seeing Danny every time she turned around.

There it was, such sadness on Diana's face. "Don't do that, Evie. I know you think things are about as bad as they can be, and honestly, Jed and I are concerned with what may or may not have happened with Danny, but we know for a fact how much he cares about you."

She pressed her hands to the tabletop, needing to end this discussion even though she wanted to ask Diana a hundred questions about Danny, what he'd do, what he thought, where he was. She couldn't do that to herself. It was like driving into an impending train wreck, so she shook her head again. "I know he does, but that's not the issue. I'm not the kind of girl who can sit on the sidelines while he decides who he wants."

She wanted to take it back, as Diana's blue eyes bored into her. They were just like Danny's, the same intensity.

"I don't know what Danny said to you, Evie, but I want you to listen to me good and hear me. I knew for a while you had feelings for Danny. You may not have been willing to admit it to yourself or to Danny, and I know the closeness you and Danny have shared, the buddies you've been. You've become a man and a woman, yet your friendship has stayed so strong. And Danny…I know my son well. He's got a good heart and a good head on his shoulders, and he's reliable and smart, but I could give him a kick in the ass for not seeing what he has with you right in front of him. I've seen for a while that he's loved you, though he may think it's just as a friend. Whatever this was that happened the other day, whatever both his father and I heard you two talking about…" Diana stopped talking, and Evie had to place both hands over her face to hide the blush. She realized his mom knew, and of course she did, because hadn't she blurted it out from the open window of her truck in her anger and frustration? She felt Diana's hand on her wrist, pulling, and she peeked through her fingers.

"I have a pretty good idea of what happened, and maybe Danny hasn't yet admitted it to himself, but he and you…" Diana pressed her hands together. "He just hasn't admitted to himself that his love for you as a friend has evolved into something deeper." She scooted back the chair. "So the job, think about it," she said, then started to the door.

Evie just sat there and listened as Diana started the pickup and drove away, thinking of the job, the offer, and what she'd said about Danny. As much as she wanted it to be true and to believe that Diana was right, she knew better. Danny may have been confused on some things, but she'd also seen how he was with Char-lie, and the fact he had to give it consideration told her everything.

Chapter Thirteen

Danny had kicked the box at the bottom of the stairs in the barn and hit concrete, and the leather of his boots hadn't quite protected him from that sharp jab. He swore and took a second, listening to the nickering of horses in the early morning light. He should have grabbed a coffee to go instead of just downing the cereal, but then he'd tossed and turned most of the night after giving up studying, having read the same chapter three times without figuring out what it said.

"You running late this morning?" His dad came out of one of the stalls and latched the gate, looking at him.

"Yes—no, I have a spare first class, but I wanted to get in early and try to get some studying in." He still needed to talk to Charlie, since he'd left after dinner three nights ago without that talk. She'd slid her body against him, her arms around his neck, and kissed him long and deep. It was nice, and he should have wanted it to go further, but at the same time it wasn't her he realized he was seeing himself with.

"Can't say I've ever seen you this rattled," His dad said, resting his forearms on the stall gate and glancing to the mare, who hung her head over as he rubbed her neck. "This is something only a girl can do. You figure anything out?"

"Yeah, I don't know. Why do I have to decide on anyone? You know, it's like, I'm at dinner, and I'm feeling myself being dragged down the aisle to make a commitment to a girl when I've been out, what, two, three times? She's great and fun and…"

His dad glanced his way but said nothing.

"I spoke to Evie," Danny said. He let out a sigh and felt as if he'd cracked open his chest and yanked out his heart from the hurt he'd seen in her face, then the way she'd walked away. "I think I made it worse."

His dad kicked at something on the barn floor. "You tell her how you feel?" He patted the horse again and faced Danny, his one arm leaning on the stall. He gave him all his attention.

"I tried, you know. I told her I needed some time just to figure out some things, and there's Charlie. I told her as well I need to figure things out, and you should have seen Evie's face. The moment I said it, I wanted to take it back, but at the same time, I couldn't lie to her, because that wouldn't be fair."

His dad glanced to the ground and then back up to him, squinting as if the sun were in his eyes. "You tell a woman you're thinking of another, what kind of reaction do you think you're going to get?"

"So, what, are you saying I should have lied to her? I don't know what I want."

His dad was shaking his head. "Well, therein lies the problem, because if you don't know what you want, who you want, you can't expect her to hang around and wait until you figure it out. You're old enough, Danny, to know, especially when you have feelings like this for a woman, if you've got a future with her or you don't. If you're really struggling to think of who it is you want beside you in your future, then maybe it's neither, but toying with both and letting them both think they have a chance with you..." His dad paused, and instead of feeling better, Danny felt like absolute crap.

"Well, that's the thing, Dad. Evie told me pretty much to get lost. She wasn't waiting around and took herself out of the equation, which I deserved. I haven't been able to get her out of my head."

His dad said nothing as he stared at him. From that look, the intensity, he knew his dad wouldn't give him the answer or tell him what he needed to do. He wasn't going to help him out, and instead he took a step over to him and rested his hand on his shoulder. "Well, that's a shame," his dad said. "You should know that your mom stopped by to see Evie the other day and offered her a job."

Danny was hit with a wave of joy for a moment, a chance of something. Just the thought of seeing her and having her working around him all the time, being there when he drove in... Then his dad's expression changed.

"She called your mom yesterday and turned her down," he said.

His heart sank.

His dad squeezed his shoulder and then walked out of the barn, calling back over his shoulder, "You'd better get going or you'll be late."

The entire drive to school, Danny fought the burning ache. It was huge, this loss that seemed to rip apart his insides. For the first time in his life, he didn't have a clue what to do. The fact was that he was starting to realize that Evie likely hated him in a way he couldn't blame her for, and the thought of not having her in his life didn't fill him with just sadness; it was a loss so deep he wondered whether he'd ever get past it. Then there was Charlie. She wasn't quite the airhead he'd thought she was, and he liked her, but that was it. Not seeing her again didn't fill him with that same heartache. He thought of her dazzling some big city, setting Chicago on fire, but he didn't see himself with her.

He pulled into the parking lot and climbed out of his Bronco, then locked the door and slung his leather back-pack over his shoulder.

"Danny…" It was Charlie in her sports car, shades on, the top down. "Just wait up," she said, then pulled in and parked two spots down.

Danny walked over to her car as she put up the top and then stepped out, locking the door. She pressed her hand to his chest and went to kiss him when he gripped her wrist gently and stepped back. "I'm sorry," he said and took in the moment she understood what he was saying. He shook his head and smiled at her.

"Danny, really?"

He touched her cheek and chin, seeing the perfection, the flawless skin, the beauty that any guy would love to have hanging off his arm. "You're beautiful, gorgeous, and are likely going to do all kinds of great things, but…"

"Not with you," she finished for him. She was about to convince him, or try to, so he shook his head.

"Charlie, I belong here. This is the life I want, and when I dream of my future and happiness, I don't see it all, but what I do see is being here, and Evie is a part of that. I'm sorry," he said. He wouldn't have been surprised if she'd yelled at him or maybe slapped his face, but instead she just shrugged and made a face as she stepped away.

"Well, then I guess you've made your choice and saved me from giving up a piece of myself and what I wanted. You know I would have thrown Chicago away for you."

He took in Charlie, seeing who she was and knowing that this life here, his life and what he wanted, was exactly the kind of life she didn't.

"You would have been miserable," he said.

She stepped back and nodded, then turned and started walking toward the campus. Now he just needed to talk to Evie, get her to listen to him, to give him a chance.

If he had to, he'd even grovel.

Chapter Fourteen

"You sure you want to do this?" Bill asked Evie. His dark hair was in bad need of a cut, but then, they'd all let everything go as of late. The lines at the sides of his eyes had deepened, but his worry seemed to have lessened overnight, since her parents had decided to give up the battle and close the barbecue restaurant down for good. Her dad was returning to butchering, and for now he was putting his dream of something bigger on hold. Evie was hopping a Greyhound to Oklahoma to see her sister Paige, get her head screwed on straight, and find something there that would give her some meaning.

A job would help, an actual check, and then she'd see whatever else happened, but sometimes distance was the best thing to heal a broken heart.

"You know what, Dad? This is exactly what I want to do, and there'll be more options there for me. Sometimes change is a good thing. Don't worry. You and Mom take care." She hugged her dad again, and he lifted his hand as she boarded the bus.

Her bags already loaded underneath, she found a seat halfway to the back at the window. Evie stuck her purse on the other seat so no one else would join her and then leaned her head against the window and listened to the rumble as the bus started and the doors closed. The bus pulled away, and instead of being happy, she wanted to weep, because she was leaving behind not just her best friend but, she realized, the love of her life. Only now could she admit it to herself, and she couldn't stick around and wait for him to figure out what he wanted only to watch him date and get close to someone else. It was cruel, and she couldn't tell him how much she wanted him, because she saw how freaked out he was.

The bus jerked and slammed its brakes, and she heard a horn honk. The door opened, and the driver was yelling at someone. Then there were footsteps.

"Evie!"

Her feet hit the floor, and she sat up, seeing Danny on the bus. What the hell? She was about to scoot down and hide when he saw her and started her way, turning to the driver.

"She's right here," he said.

Then the driver was saying something to Danny, and Evie didn't know what to do or say. For the first time in her life, she was speechless.

"You were going to run out on me," he said, and a slow smile touched his face.

She knew she was staring like a fool. "Uh, Danny, not sure what this is…" She looked around, taking in all the curious faces.

"We're on a schedule here," the driver called out. "I need you to get off the bus."

Danny just stared at Evie and shook his head. "Not without my girl," he said.

"Danny, what the hell are you doing?" She gritted her teeth. "I'm going to Oklahoma, and..."

He was shaking his head. "You're running out on me is what you're doing."

"Ma'am, are you staying or getting off the bus?" the driver said, and Evie didn't know where to look.

"Danny, you need to get off the bus," she said. "I told you already—"

"You need to forgive me for not seeing that you were right in front of me," he said. "Don't leave, Evie. We've been friends for a lot of years, and I've loved you, but what I didn't want to admit was the fact that I love you not just as a friend but as something more. When I think of my future, imagining it without you, it's darkness and nothingness. You in my future is what I want, the only way I want it."

Evie was taking in the faces around her, and an older woman across from her was gesturing to Danny.

"If you don't go with him, I will," the woman said.

This was crazy, and Evie was suddenly standing. Danny had her purse and was herding her down the steps. The driver followed, and she gestured to her bags underneath. He pulled them out and dumped them on the sidewalk. She didn't need to look up to know that everyone on the bus was watching them, her. Then Danny had her bags, the driver was in the bus, and it was pulling away.

Danny tossed her bags in his Bronco, which she hadn't noticed. It was pulled in at an odd angle ahead of where the bus was parked.

"Danny, this is crazy. You can't just pull me off a bus and say the things you did to me and expect me to—"

"Shut up," he snapped, and she wanted to take a step back as he slid his hands over her cheeks and stepped closer. "I have something to say to you, and I want you to listen to me. I love you, Evie Wetzel, and I don't know what's going to happen in the future or what problems or obstacles or crazy hours or lost sleep will happen as I work for my law degree, but what I do know is that I have loved you and I couldn't even admit it to myself, and I want you beside me through all of this." He pressed a kiss to her lips, and he was still holding her face.

She rested her hands on his wrists, reeling from what he was saying. "And Charlie?" she said, but he was shaking his head.

"I'm sorry, she's not who I want. It's you, and I couldn't even admit it. I thought I was being honest with you when in fact I was lying to myself."

She stepped back and pulled away, letting Danny's hand fall. This was crazy. "Danny, you can't expect me to just drop everything and stay, and…" She was leaving because she couldn't stand the thought of seeing him with another woman, but she needed a job still.

"You were running away," he stated.

She was going to deny it, but then he went down on one knee on the sidewalk, and she was in horror, watching. "Danny, what the hell are you doing? People are watching. Get up!"

But he wouldn't. In fact, he reached for her hand, and she took in the faces of strangers, amused and watching.

"Evie, I've loved you forever, and I can't imagine a

future without you. I don't want a future without you. Will you marry me?"

She felt her jaw slacken, and she stared at Danny as if he'd lost his mind. Then she realized he didn't care who was watching them as he waited for her to say something. "Get up right now," she whispered loudly.

A smile touched his lips as he stood, and his eyes filled with the sparkle that had made her fall in love with him.

"Danny, this is crazy. You're in school, and I don't have a job…" She saw that he was waiting, and she gestured again at him, at a loss for words.

He lifted his hand and ran it over her chin, stepping closer. "Evie…" he prompted her, and she just stared into those deep, intensely blue eyes, which she could have spent a lifetime looking at.

"Okay," she finally said, and then she was in his arms.

He was swinging her around, and she slid down his body as his lips found hers out there on that sidewalk in downtown North Lakewood where everyone could see.

When he let her down, his arms still around her, she said, "You know I don't have a job."

He steered her to his Bronco. "Funny thing about that. Since you're going to be part of my family, there's this little job that happens to have your name on it with my mom and dad, where we're going to be living on the ranch." He had lifted her into the passenger side of the Bronco, and he leaned in and kissed her again.

"You just asked me to marry you so I'd take the job and you can keep me around," she teased, then smiled.

"Yeah, you just keep telling yourself that, Evie," he said. Then he kissed her again.

Chapter Fifteen

"You're getting married?"

The way his parents stared at him as he stood with Evie outside the house, Danny could have sworn they thought he'd lost his mind. He was holding her hand, halfway to the barn, where his mom and dad had been lingering as they'd driven in.

His dad was now looking at his mom, whose hair was pulled up in a messy bun, with smudges of dirt on her cheek. She was staring from Evie to him as if the shock of what he'd said hadn't quite sunk in.

"I asked Evie, and she said yes," Danny said. He glanced to Evie, still unable to believe it. She was now appearing shell shocked, or he thought so, anyway. He nudged her, and startled brown eyes stared up at him. Yup, his parents were likely freaking her out.

"Well," Evie said, "truth of the matter is that he ambushed me on the bus. With the drama he created, he left me no choice but to get off even though I was packed and ready to leave the state, start somewhere new. Everyone was still watching us and could hear what we were saying as he got down on one knee in the middle of town, on the sidewalk…"

Was Evie saying she didn't want to get married?

"Can you give us a second?" Danny said and pulled her away over to his Bronco, leaving his parents standing where they were, speechless. Actually, the expression on their faces was one he'd never seen before. "Don't you want to get married?" he asked and took in Evie's wide eyes.

"Honestly, since having a moment to think about everything, I'm wondering if you asked me to marry you just to keep me here. If that's the case, then you should know I'm not interested, and I'm giving you an out right now. Just say the word, tell me you kind of overreacted and didn't really think it all the way through, and I'll completely understand."

Was she serious? He stared down at her and over to his parents, who were talking, maybe finally having gotten past the shock of what he'd said. "Evie, if I didn't want to marry you, I wouldn't have asked. Look, maybe it seems rushed…"

Her eyes widened.

He was still holding one of her hands, and he reached for the other. "But what I said to you, I meant it. I want a future with you, and I'm not saying it'll be easy. It will likely mean we have to make some adjustments, but make no mistake: I want you, and when it's right…"

She stared at him before a slow smile eased across her face. "Okay," she said and shrugged, and he pulled her close and kissed her before she could add anything else. She was quiet and looking a little stunned when he pulled away. He'd have to remember that kissing Evie was how to quiet her smart mouth.

"Yes, we're getting married!" he shouted, linking his fingers with Evie's again and pulling her back over to his parents.

"Well," his mom said, "I have to say this isn't what I expected, Danny. Evie…" She gestured between them, and this was the first time Danny had seen her speechless. His dad, though, was looking at him with an expression that bordered on amusement. Then Jed shook his head as if again considering whether Danny had lost his mind.

"Look, I realize we're young, and I'm still in school, but this is perfect," Danny said. "We'll get married, and Evie will help out here. The job you offered her, Mom? She'll take it, and we'll live in the loft for now. Then with law school next year, we'll figure it out," he said. Law school meant Seattle, and he hadn't considered anything other than dorm living, but they could rent a small place. Evie could get a job there easily, and they'd be together. What else mattered?

Jed crossed his arms over his chest. "So when are you planning on getting married, then?"

"Well, we haven't decided, but I'm thinking before summer, two weeks?" Danny said. He took in Evie, who was now frowning and shaking her head. He'd thrown it out there without having had a chance to discuss anything with her.

"You want to get married in two weeks?" she said. "I still have to tell my parents, and how are we supposed to make a wedding happen that quickly, and where? Paying for a venue is out of the question. I can't ask my mom and dad for anything. They don't have a spare dime."

He could hear the panic she wasn't trying to hide.

Diana, who was staring from him to Evie, threw her hands up in the air. "That's a simple fix. You have the wedding here, we decide on what you want, and we keep it simple, no cost. Evie, why don't you and I discuss the wedding details, since Danny likely has no idea what it takes to put a wedding together? Danny, I think your dad wants to have a word with you." His mom actually reached over and grabbed Evie's wrist to pull her toward the house. She looked back once, wide eyed, questioning, but Danny just watched. The girl he'd known forever was now going to be his wife, and everything he'd considered and planned in the past few hours seemed to converge on him. For a minute, he wanted to sit down.

Maybe his dad knew, as he rested his hand on his shoulder. "Well, I suppose that was one way to handle it, Danny, tossing a marriage proposal out there," he said, and Danny wondered whether his dad was going to laugh at him or lecture him. "Was that what you really wanted, or was it all you could think of to keep Evie here?"

He hadn't thought of that. When he'd stopped by her house instead of going to class, which he was so glad he'd done, her mom had said she was on her way to Oklahoma. Yes, he'd panicked a bit over losing her. The thought that he'd driven her away had made him race into town to stop her before she got on the bus, but the bus had already been pulling out, and, well, he'd just reacted. "I didn't plan it," he said. "I just got her off the bus, and I asked her. It just came out."

The look his dad was now leveling on him seemed to hint at a coming lecture. "That's not why you ask a woman to marry you, Danny. When I said to think about what you want and who you want, this isn't what I meant. Marriage is a big step, and even though you and Evie have known each other forever, better than most couples, are you sure marriage is something you're ready for? It's a big step up from being friends. It's kind of like you skipped right over dating."

Danny just looked at the house, where Evie had disappeared with his mom. "Dad, why are you trying to put doubts in my head?" he said. The last thing he wanted now was to go to Evie and say, *Oops, my bad! Let's try dating first and slow it down.*

"I'm not trying to put doubts in your head, but if you're having them, now is the time to say something."

He just stared at the house again. Christopher, his brother, was coming out. He was in his senior year, also with bright red hair, wearing a ball cap and worn jeans, obviously going for a ride or something. He walked right over to Danny.

"Mom's inside and said you and Evie are getting married." Christopher wasn't smiling but instead had the same look as his dad, as if he too thought Danny was crazy.

"We are, and no, Dad, I have no doubts. I'm absolutely one hundred percent sure about marrying Evie. The sooner the better, and with Evie now here where I want her, she can also take that job Mom offered, helping out here. She's a part of the family from here on out."

Christopher just shrugged, reached over, and slapped Danny's shoulder before he kept walking to the barn. "Cool. I like Evie" was all he said.

"It isn't cool!" Jed called out over his shoulder, but

Christopher only turned and laughed. His dad was shaking his head as he faced him again. "You still need to talk to Evie's parents."

Danny said nothing for a minute, because he'd forgotten about them and the fact that they thought their daughter was on her way to Oklahoma, long gone from North Lakewood. "Yeah, I guess we should do it sooner rather than later."

Jed just inclined his head. "Sooner would be best, considering the gossips in this town. Do it before someone else tells them first, don't you think?"

In the distance, up the long driveway from the highway, Danny saw dust trailing an approaching car. It was coming closer by the second, an older Buick. "Oh shit," he said just as he felt his dad's hand on his shoulder.

"You got that right," Jed said just as Evie's parents pulled in. "You'd better go get her."

Chapter Sixteen

"Okay, I'm going to say it," Diana said. "I've been hoping for a lot of years that you two would figure out how perfect you'd be together, and the fact you have makes me very happy—even springing a wedding on us, which I didn't see coming. If any two can do it, I have absolute faith you and Danny can, but honestly, again, I didn't expect it to happen quite yet, maybe a year or two down the road..."

She was making tea and had set out cookies on a plate. She put china cups on the now cleared kitchen table along with some napkins. Christopher and Mark had walked through the dining room, both grabbing cookies and taking a second to absorb what their mom had said, then walked away as if it was nothing. Christopher had headed out the front door, Mark to his room at the back of the house, and Evie sat there in a hard-back chair, trying to figure out why Diana was setting up what looked like a tea party. Maybe she and Danny had interrupted some meeting Diana was planning.

Evie just stared at Diana, who was walking back and

forth to the kitchen, filling the table with milk, sugar, spoons, and a stack of luncheon plates.

"And I'll finally get to have a daughter, yeah!" Diana said and rested her hand on Evie's shoulder, patting it. She seemed far too happy, and Evie didn't know what to say, since this wasn't what she'd expected. "So let's talk wedding, what you want. After all, it's your day. What would make you happy and be the perfect day for you, Evie? What about the flowers, everything…"

Diana was in the kitchen again when the front door opened, and there was Danny, followed by her parents. *Oh no!*

"Hi, Mom, Dad," Evie said. "By the looks on your faces, I see you heard. Yay, surprise! Getting married."

Oh, wow, that sounded pathetic. Danny's expression at her smart mouth said it all, the way he stared at her. She wondered what her parents had said to him. Jed followed them in and closed the door, and the tension ratcheted up the energy in the room.

"Well, honestly, we're trying to figure out what happened," said her mom. "Your father dropped you off at the bus, and then Audrey Clayton is coming through the door of the dry cleaners to inform me she saw Danny propose to you in the middle of town on the sidewalk, getting down on one knee in front of everyone, and that was after the scene he apparently caused while stopping the bus and getting you off."

Marion Wetzel was who Evie had gotten her hair and height from. Her eyes were her dad's, though. Bill stood a few inches taller than her mom but was still a short man compared to Danny and Jed.

"I guess I'm not clear on how and why, considering I thought you were dating someone else," Bill said to

Danny, who appeared beside Evie where she sat. Okay, so her parents were a little shell shocked.

Danny rested his hand on her shoulder, which was much appreciated, because this was the first time she'd ever felt this lost for words. His hand, as it squeezed, was full of support. "Evie is who I want, not anyone else. That wasn't anything serious. So to answer all your questions, yes, we are getting married, and yes, I got down on one knee in front of the town and proposed, and Evie said yes."

Her mom's jaw slackened, and her mouth gaped. Evie hadn't seen her mom this shocked since her sister Paige, who was now married in Oklahoma, had told them she was pregnant before they'd even met the father. Her dad had a blank expression, but it was likely he didn't have a clue what to say.

"The kids here are talking two weeks," Jed added as he stepped around them, putting his hand on her dad's shoulder first. Her dad's expression was priceless.

"What's the rush? Seriously, are you pregnant?" Marion said.

"Oh my God, Mom, no. I am not." She was mortified and felt Danny's hands, both of them, press into her shoulders as if holding her back.

"We don't want to wait," he said. "We've known each other forever, and she's the one."

Diana was holding her iPad, standing in the center of the room, and Evie thought she was doing a fine job ignoring the shock from her parents. "Well, a Saturday two weeks from now is actually ten days," she said. "We're already talking about having it here and keeping it simple, so there's virtually no cost for the venue."

Evie could see Diana was trying to make it easier for

her parents, considering she had to know the dire financial strain they were under. She wasn't about to ask her parents to cough up anything.

"Come and sit down," Diana said. "I made tea."

There were cups for six, as if Diana had known they were coming. Then they were sitting, Jed at the end, reaching for a cookie. Danny sat beside her, and then her mom burst into tears.

"Mom, seriously," Evie said. Bill was rubbing Marion's shoulder as if he'd expected her emotion.

"Oh, this has just been a rough few months with closing the restaurant, and now you're getting married," she said. "How are we supposed to plan a proper wedding in such a short amount of time? You need a dress, and there's flowers, and what about the food? And we need music and dancing."

Evie could feel her eyes widening and wondered why her dad wasn't freaking out. The way her mom was talking, it would cost a fortune, and she didn't want that. "You know what? We don't need to have all that…" she started, but the way her mom and Diana stared her down, she let the words fall away.

"Of course you do," Diana said, "and there's a way for us to make it all happen on a budget." She took a seat and poured tea into Marion's cup, then Evie's, before sliding the teapot in front of Danny. He seemed to get what his mom wanted, as next he was standing and filling everyone's cup.

"You know, Mom, I'm not looking for anything crazy," he said, "and I'm sure Evie doesn't want anything too upscale either. Let's just keep it low key. We can get a justice of the peace to show up here, a few friends, and we can have a barbecue here after, throw some burgers on, beer. That's it."

Evie was holding her steaming cup of tea. Frankly, his idea sounded great, but at the same time, she took in the way his mom and hers were frowning and staring at her to say something. She shrugged. "Simple is good, and—" She stopped when Diana reached over and touched her hand, which she pressed to the table after putting down her teacup.

"What my son is talking about is great for a get together or a weekend with friends, not a wedding. No, ten days isn't a lot of time, but we can do better than that."

As her mom and Diana looked at each other, Evie felt the situation slipping from her control. She glanced over to Danny, who was now standing by his dad, saying nothing. She knew he too realized the moment their simple wedding had been taken over by their moms.

Chapter Seventeen

Not only was Evie not living with Danny in his loft, but she'd been tucked into the back of her parents' Buick when they'd driven away after two hours of discussion about how their wedding could and would shape out. Bill had insisted on handling the food, a barbecue of sorts, and they'd agreed to just the immediate family and some close friends. Jed was going to talk to a local group of guys he knew who often played at the community dances.

If the weather was good, the tables would be outside, a tent on hand. Then there was the issue of sourcing the wine and beer and he didn't know what else. It seemed as if their simple wedding was being transformed into anything but.

Danny now had his books open in front of him, sitting at his small round table in his loft. He'd missed an entire day of classes, and he was getting married in ten days. "The rings! Oh no," he said out loud as he rubbed his forehead.

He heard a knock on the door at the bottom of the stairs, then footsteps.

"Danny?" Jed called out as he started walking up. His boots clattered on the steps.

Danny said nothing as he rested his arm on the books, wondering what kind of ring Evie would like. She wasn't the flashy kind of girl who needed glitz and glamor and everything his pocketbook wouldn't allow. Charlie would have insisted on a rock the size of a mountain. It was an image that didn't fit Evie, and thankfully so. That was another reason he was relieved at his choice. He could understand now what his dad had meant about who he belonged with.

Danny looked over to his dad, who was now taking in the loft, the mess, the pile of clothes on his bed, and the covers tossed in a heap. He should have made it, and he needed to try to get some studying in.

"You didn't say much after Bill and Marion left with Evie. Neither of you did, for that matter," Jed said as he walked over to where Danny was sitting. "Guess you and Evie should be comfortable enough here." Then he was standing in front of him, looking at him as if waiting for him to say something.

"We will," he said and just nodded, wishing Evie were there. He'd not even had a moment to speak with her about moving in with him, because with the emotion and excitement of the day with their parents, he hadn't found an opportune time. How exactly would his parents feel about it? "So I was thinking of having Evie move in here now, before the wedding," he said.

His dad stared at him with one of his unreadable expressions before glancing over to the bed. He cleared his throat. "You think Bill Wetzel would be okay with that? Because I don't. Can't see him allowing it, and with the fact that you've kind of sprung this marriage thing on all of us, I'd say the best advice I can give you right now is wait. Best not to get off on the wrong foot with your future father-in-law, considering Evie still lives under their roof. Besides, this may be the time the both of you need to figure out some things."

What his dad meant by that, he didn't know, so he just stared up at him. "Like…?" he prompted, waiting his dad out as a slow, easy smile touched his lips.

His mom had mentioned on more than a few occasions that Jed was the strong, silent type, much like Danny. It was a quality that drove her batty at times, or so she said, and now Danny was on the receiving end of it. He didn't much care for it.

"Well, Evie is here in the morning to work for us, taking a lot of the day-to-day handling of this place off all our shoulders, or as much of it as we can convince her to handle. You'll be off to school, and you have exams this week, but then you're done. Then you start law school in the fall. You have very few days until you and Evie get married. Use that time to get some things settled between the two of you, because you've suddenly gone from best friends to a very different type of relationship. Spend the days until the wedding going through everything. Figure out whether Evie'll be living here and where you're going to live in Seattle, and then talk about everything in between. For example, on the weekends, when you're not in school, are you settling in Seattle permanently, or will you be coming back here? How are you going to handle the money, paying for everything? Even though your mom and I have paid for school for you, there are still other things you and Evie need to discuss. Come to an understanding with each other, because now the entire dynamic has changed."

Danny was staring at his dad, trying to make sense of all of it, because that was the most his dad had ever said. He wasn't much of a talker. It was his mom who took care of all that. "Well, Evie and I haven't had much of a chance to talk about it, but I planned on Evie getting work in Seattle. We'll find a place to rent there. I'm not looking for a handout, Dad. Evie and I will figure it out. I know it won't be easy, but I can pick up something part time, as well," he added, feeling a giant pressure in his chest. Maybe this was the price of responsibility.

An easy smile made its way to his dad's amber eyes, and Danny wondered whether he found what he'd said to be funny. "That's quite the plan, and that's quite the ambition you have, and admirable, too, but how about a reality check? Rent won't be cheap there, and with school taking all day every day and you trying to pick up part-time work, how often will you and Evie likely see each other?" He was shaking his head. "You should see your face right now. That there is what I'm talking about. When you're married, the responsibility will fall on you to look after your wife, your family…" Jed stepped around the table, placing both palms flat on it, looking at Danny closely. "That thing you're feeling right now will never go away," he said. Then he walked over to the stairs and looked back at him. "You scared yet?"

For a minute he didn't know how to answer. Then he shook his head. "No, of course not."

He swallowed, feeling his palms sweat, thinking of

the ring he needed to buy and Evie moving in, being with him always. Now it wasn't just about him.

His dad's lips tugged to the side in a twitch that seemed to say he was having a lot of fun at Danny's expense. "You should be," he said.

Danny just watched as his dad went down the steps and started whistling a tune that had the hair at the back of his neck standing up.

Chapter Eighteen

"So, as you can see, Jed is about the worst manager there is," Diana said. "You don't need to be an academic to know what needs to be done. Handling all this, it's almost the same as everything you did for your dad's restaurant. Instead of making sure you have the supplies you need, cashing out, doing up a bank deposit, and waiting on hungry customers of all types, you're simply making sure the feed for the horses arrives, reminding Jed when the hay needs to be reordered, handling the correspondence, and reminding parents who are behind on their fees to pay up. When all the bills come in, you can't let Jed just toss them in a pile someplace to be forgotten about. Let me tell you, my husband never remembers orders. He tacks a Post-it somewhere no one can find it and is better at letting everyone have credit. The number of parents we, or rather I, have to chase after to pay every month takes a lot of time away from everything else."

Diana was such a beautiful woman even when dressed down, as she was now, in a faded T-shirt of her husband's over old blue jeans, her hair pulled up in a messy bun. She was one of those women who were so gorgeous she could do nothing to downplay it.

"So what if one of the parents won't pay?" Evie said. "Do you cut their kid from riding?" She didn't want to play the heavy, but she'd dealt with worse at the barbecue: rude travelers, rowdies who'd had one beer too many, and once an overstressed mom who'd tried to get everything she could for free.

Diana stared at her, deep blue eyes weighing the question. Then she took a deep breath and slowly shook her head. "No, unfortunately, Jed and I could never do that to a child, considering all these kids have some type of special need. Just do your best…" She reached over and pressed her hand over Evie's. "I guarantee you that alone is already better than both me and Jed could do. I'm relieved just having you here. You have no idea what you're taking off my shoulders and Jed's."

Evie heard a vehicle and glanced out from the small office at the back of the barn where she'd been with Diana for the past hour, going through files, a mess of papers that Diana had happily passed over to her so she could bring order to this chaos.

"Danny's home," Diana said, poking her head out just as Evie heard the rattle and loud roar from what sounded like her own truck. They both stepped out of the office to see Jed slip out of Danny's Bronco. Danny was behind the wheel of her truck, having picked her up early before school and taken her keys from her before kissing her briefly and driving away.

"I can hear they picked up my truck," she said. She'd meant it to be a joke, and she took in the amusement in Diana's expression.

"The gas tank was dry," called out Jed, her future father-in-law.

Diana slid her arm over Evie's shoulder. "And here it starts. See what you have to look forward to?"

Evie was suddenly unsettled, because Danny had also said he wanted to have a talk with her about their current living situation after he finished his classes. The engine of her truck was steaming, and Danny had the hood open. She watched as father and son looked at the mess under the hood, which was tied together with wire and glue. Well, it plugged up all the leaks, anyway.

"So you filled it with gas, and…"

The way Jed was staring at her and Danny was frowning, it seemed as if they'd discussed a lot, and it was all about her and the heap of metal she was rather attached to, considering it was all she'd been able to afford. The time she'd put into it to keep it running had her taking in the rust bucket with a lot of fondness.

"Dad had a gas can and met me at your parents' place," Danny said, his forearm resting on the lip of the truck. "But, seriously, taking a look at this, we can replace the hose, but not sure it's worth fixing it up to keep it running."

Jed held a rag and was looking in the oil reservoir, shaking his head. "You'd need a pile of work on this, Evie. Sometimes it's best to give it up. What it'll cost in parts alone, it may be cheaper and better to just pick up something else, take this to the wreckers. Looking at this, I'm wondering about its roadworthiness."

She could feel the way Diana's hand gripped her shoulder. "Awe, I don't know, Jed," Diana said. She was happy, teasing. "This truck kind of looks like the one you had when we first met."

Danny was still poking around under her hood. Diana walked away, following Jed around her truck. Evie stepped up beside Danny. He was so tall and big, even leaning against her truck. He pulled his attention away from her grimy engine and looked over to her. There it was, those vibrant eyes, and he leaned in and pressed a kiss to her lips, so nice. She felt her face warm, knowing his parents were there. She allowed her hand to slip to his cheek, and when he pulled away, he was watching her, seeing her discomfort.

"I want you to move in here," he said, and she just stared for a second at him, trying to figure out what he was saying.

"But I'll be…"

He shook his head. "I mean now, not after the wedding—tonight."

She understood then. Of course she wanted to, but her reaction was filled with panic. "Danny, I can't yet. It's…" She glanced over her shoulder, hearing Diana and Jed coming back around the truck. Suddenly, just being there seemed really uncomfortable, but then Danny slid his arm around her and had her walking with him. "Danny, what are you doing?"

He was holding her hand now, pulling her along. "Taking you someplace we can talk alone," he said.

Evie glanced back, seeing Diana watching them, but Jed was now looking under the hood again, not paying them any mind, or maybe he didn't think much of the fact that Danny was dragging her away.

Danny had her at the stairs to his loft and was pressing his hand to the small of her back, leading her in. She started up the steps, hearing the door close at the bottom.

"Danny, that was kind of rude," she said.

His hand skimmed over her butt, giving it a light smack as she hurried up the steps to the top, the sound of their footsteps clattering. She took in the loft, open and airy, with a pine finish and a small kitchenette on one side, a queen bed unmade against the wall. The other side had a deep brown sofa with a flat-screen TV on the wall.

Danny had her in his arms, pulling her against him. He lowered his head and pressed his lips to hers, angling her head with his hands, holding her and controlling the kiss. He tasted her, and she could feel him pulling her up as she stood on her tip toes, his hands pressing her into him, holding her so close. It was exciting, and her arms slid around his neck, holding on to him as he had his way with her. She could have spent a lifetime kissing him, letting him touch her like this, rocking with him.

Somehow, he moved her back, and she felt the bed press against her legs, the backs of her knees. She was now lying down, and he was on top of her, his hands running down her sides, over her butt, pulling her shirt free from her jeans and working on the buttons. At the same time, her hands were pulling at his faded T-shirt, lifting it and feeling the warm skin underneath. As hers fell open, his hands settled over her small breasts in the very practical bra she wore.

He pulled back and lifted off his shirt, and for a minute she felt so exposed, but staring at his broad chest, so smooth, she was dying to run her hands over his perfection, to feel him pressed against her. The thought of waking up to that every morning hit her, and she had to struggle to breathe. Then he was back and had her shirt off, her bra pulled free. She knew the moment his lips touched hers where this was headed, and it was happening way too fast.

"Danny, we need to talk about some things…" she started as he kissed her neck and lower, and she hissed as his mouth settled over her breasts, tasting her. She pressed her head back into the mattress as she felt his leg settle in between hers. She could feel his strength, the muscles in his thighs as his hand skimmed over all of her, feeling every part of her, fast and furious. She could feel him pressing into her, and the size of him was drowning that rational part of her that wanted to talk, because now she was so warm and wanting him that she was battling the need to pull him closer. Her head was losing the ability to reason and slow him down…

"Danny?" His dad knocked on the door and yanked it open, and she thought she shrieked.

Danny pulled back but didn't get off her. "Later! We're kind of busy," he called out, and Evie wanted to smack his shoulder.

She pressed her hands to his chest and pushed. "Off now!" she whispered loudly, freaking out as she heard a footstep and wondered whether Jed was on his way up. Her eyes searched for her shirt, but she only saw his T-shirt there on the floor at her feet, so she reached for it and pulled it over her head.

Seeing the open bathroom door as her escape, she ran to it and slammed it shut behind her.

Chapter Nineteen

Danny just stared at the closed door of the bathroom and then over to the railing, knowing his dad was standing at the bottom. He wanted to snarl, considering his discomfort and the timing. He stepped closer to the rail and looked down, his hand running over his bare chest, taking in the amusement staring up from the bottom of the stairs. "Maybe I should get a lock for that door," he said.

"Timing, Danny. Remember what I said?" Jed asked.

Danny took in the meaning, wanting to curse at his misery but also realizing what his dad was getting at. He said nothing as he stared, and his dad lifted his hand as he started back out the door.

"Oh, I just stopped to tell you your mom is driving me over to Evie's parents' place to pick up my truck. I was going to see if Evie wanted to come now. We'd drop her off at home."

There it was, his dad's sense of humor.

"I'll take Evie home, so you take your time," Danny

said and waited as his dad hesitated before stepping out and then closing the door. Danny took a breath and a minute to just listen to the quiet, hearing nothing from the bathroom. He heard a vehicle start. It had to be his mom's new SUV, and then it was pulling away, and with it went the sizeable pressure of having his space invaded.

"Are you going to hide out in there all day?" he called out and waited as the door opened and Evie appeared, her hair a mess, having been pulled free from the ponytail it was always hiked up into. She was wearing his shirt, which was way too big for her but looked surprisingly sexy. She stepped out, and her big brown eyes were hesitant.

"Your dad gone?" she said, holding the door and taking him in. He could see the shyness creep into her. That was something he wasn't familiar with. This was a new Evie, a side of Evie he hadn't known existed.

"Yeah, sorry about his timing," he said. What was she thinking as she stepped out closer to him? She was pulling at her arm as if she was cold, but it was anything but in the loft.

"Before I forget," he said and pulled a cell phone from his back pocket, "I got this for you. It's on my plan." He held it out to her, closing the distance between them.

She just stared at it with a look of confusion before taking a breath. "Why are you getting me a cell phone?" she said and flicked her gaze up to him.

He held the new iPhone out to her until she took it, taking it in. "Because we're getting married, and you don't have one," he said.

She tilted her head, leveling him with a gaze. "But I do have one. I just didn't pay it, remember?" She stopped talking, and he waited for her to say something else. She shrugged. "But I will," she said. Oh, how stubborn she could be.

"That's why you now have a new one, and it's under my name, and I'll pay for it. You don't have to worry anymore about anything, because I'll take care of you."

The look she gave him, he wasn't sure what to make of it. "Danny, just because we're getting married, that doesn't mean you all of a sudden need to pay for everything." She gestured at the phone, which she was still holding.

He walked closer to her and ran his hands over her arms and shoulders, just touching her as she looked up to him. "Yeah, it does, and the same goes for the truck. For now, we'll just use the Bronco. One vehicle is all we need. I'm almost done school, and then I'm here, and so are you." He slid his hand over her cheek. "I want you to move in now."

Her hand fisted and slid over her chest, and she slowly shook her head. "Danny, as much as I want to, I don't think that would be best. My parents are still kind of thrown by what happened, you proposing and all, and it's not like we have a long engagement. In fact, it's less than—"

"Nine days and counting." He cut her off because that was all he'd been able to think of.

A smile tugged at the sides of her lips. "What would it hurt to wait the nine days? I mean, it'll give me time to pack my things, move them over here, and figure out a lot of the things you and I haven't talked about. Then there are the wedding details your mom and mine seem to have taken over." She was staring at the phone and moved back over to the bed, taking in the mess, the fact that he hadn't bothered making it. That was never something he'd done. He watched as she pulled up the duvet and made the bed after setting the new phone on the side table.

"Just in case you didn't realize, Danny, we still haven't had a chance to discuss law school, how long we're staying here, and where next. The University of Washington is in Seattle, but we've never talked about how to make it work. I know you've told me more than once before about your plans to stay in a dorm, but now…" She finished straightening his bed, and it wasn't lost on him that she was still wearing his shirt as she picked up her tiny white bra and shirt from the floor. She placed them on the bed, her back to him, then glanced back at him.

He wondered what she was thinking, as he could see her shyness taking hold again. As he allowed his gaze to skim over her tiny perfection, he couldn't believe he'd never noticed his growing attraction before. "Okay, let's talk about it," he said. "We'll find an apartment close to school. There will be lots of jobs, and you'll find one easily. We can save over the next few months before we go, and with what I already have stashed and what you make here, then with the pack trips I'll help my dad with this summer, we'll have a nice little nest egg. The dorm is out of the question now since we're getting married, but finding something small shouldn't be that difficult. We'll figure it out, and if I need to, I'll pick up part-time work, too. I never said it would be easy."

He moved closer to her, and this time he lifted his hand, sliding it over her shoulder and down her arm, pulling her closer so she was leaning against him. He reached for the clothes she was clutching and gently tugged. "I don't think you're going to need these right now," he said as he leaned down, then kissed her cheek, her neck. He slid his hand back over the flat of her stomach, pulling her back against him, and turned her in his arms. "Kind of a shame you made the bed, since I'm planning on messing it up again."

When he went to kiss her again, she ducked down and slipped away, reaching for her bra and shirt on the floor. "Yeah, no. Your mom and dad will be back soon, and I'm not waiting for them to walk in here and catch us in bed next. Thank you, but no thanks. That was way too embarrassing. So…" Her hand slapped his chest as he stepped toward her, reaching for her again. "You can just cool it. Besides, I'm getting hungry. It's dinner time, and…" She looked around at his kitchen. "I think it's time you cooked me dinner." Then she scooted past him to the bathroom with her bra and shirt and pointed to the kitchen. "So you go and start, and I'm going to get dressed."

She closed the door to the bathroom, and this time he heard the lock click. "Man, this is going to be a long nine days," he muttered as he walked over to the fridge and pulled it open, seeing a carton of milk, a few beers, and half a carton of eggs. Maybe he needed to go to the store. That was something he hadn't done, not because he couldn't cook but because it was easier to walk over to his parents' place for dinner. He guessed at this point that was just one more thing that was going to have to change.

Chapter Twenty

"This is one of our top sellers, three diamonds in a fourteen-karat gold setting. It's on sale for only nine hundred and forty-eight dollars, which is a bargain, considering the quality."

Danny stared at the simple gold ring with three tiny diamonds. He couldn't believe the price tag for such a small ring. Although it was nice, it was nothing glamorous, and he was still stuck on the cost. He needed every dollar he could get for the deposit on a new place, the rent, and the essentials. That was something he still needed to sit and take a closer look at, and soon.

He was holding the tiny cute ring, leaning on the glass counter at the jewellery store. The man behind it was balding, with glasses, wearing brown tweed. He hadn't made much of an impression on Danny, and even the flashy diamond on his pinky was more of a turnoff than anything. He heard a ding from the door. "You know what? I'd like to see the wedding sets…" he started before the man gave his attention to whoever had walked in.

"I'll be right with you," he said. The practiced smile that had greeted Danny was back on the man's face.

Danny glanced to the side and straightened when Charlie stepped up beside him. She lifted her dark shades, pressing them to the top of her head. Her long dark hair was loose, and she was dressed in heels, in a deep brown silky tank dress, classy, sexy. She did nothing for him now.

"Hi, Danny. So I heard about you and Evie. Well, actually, everyone's talking about it, considering the scene you apparently caused. Rather romantic," she said, and for a minute he wasn't sure how to respond. Then she smiled that bright smile that seemed to flow from her with ease. "You finished exams? Saw you pull away from school today, and you seemed rather in a hurry."

There Charlie went again, getting in his business. Why was she there?

"I have one more tomorrow, and then I'm done," he said.

She nodded and then glanced at the ring. "May I?" She reached for it and seemed to examine it. He wasn't sure what she was thinking. When she glanced back to him, he noticed her makeup, tasteful as always, not caked on, but then, Charlie was never one to go au naturel, another thing about her that was different from Evie. He'd never seen Evie wear makeup like Charlie did. In fact, he didn't think she'd ever worn it at all.

"For Evie, I presume," she said. "It's simple and wouldn't stand out, just a mediocre ring. So you really are getting married." She was still holding the ring, and for a minute he didn't know what to say.

"We are, in a little over a week." He reached for the

ring and held it out to the jeweler, who now had pulled out the his and hers wedding sets he'd asked for. They included diamond bridal pieces, and he couldn't see the price tags, but from the way the man studied him, Danny thought he'd left the higher-ticket items tucked away. "So what do these start at?"

Charlie was still there, now leaning on the glass, looking at all the rings, obviously interested in what he was doing. Her chin rested on her palm.

"Well, if nine hundred is too steep, there are the simple gold bands, which you can never go wrong with," the salesman said. "Depending on budget, there's the ten karat, or…" The man lifted out another set, a gold band for each of them, very plain and basic. "This is as cheap as you can go. As you can see, it has no frills, gold plated, a steal at one hundred and twenty dollars." His voice was dripping with sarcasm.

"That looks just like the kind of rings my grandparents had," Charlie said. "Nothing to them. Danny, you can't seriously be considering these. A girl expects a nice ring. It's the kind of thing a man gives to the woman he loves, like that one there." Charlie tapped the glass, and Danny took in a square-cut diamond surrounded by others in rose gold. The jeweler reached for it and held it out to Charlie, who slid it on her finger. Of course, it looked amazing.

"And the cost on that? Afraid to ask," Danny said teasingly.

The man, who hadn't cracked a smile yet, just stared at Danny with disapproval. "That's a specialty diamond, one of a kind, and comes with a price tag of thirty-eight thousand nine hundred."

Charlie was still smiling, holding her hand out,

admiring the ring, not fazed at all by the price tag. Danny thought for a second that his heart had stopped beating, as a huge lump now squeezed in his chest. He realized the man was serious.

"Now this is a ring, Danny, that says she's your everything," Charlie said.

He wondered whether she had any idea of the different worlds they came from. He could almost hear his dad in the back of his head, saying, *Put the ring back!*

"So the wedding sets are simple, but…" Danny spotted a his and hers set in pink gold. Her ring had seven tiny diamonds in the band. "That one?" He pointed to them and hoped they were somewhat reasonable.

The jeweler pulled the case out and glanced at what Danny thought was the price. "Ten karat rose gold. This is from the lower end of the sweetheart collection and is on sale for two hundred and forty-nine dollars."

He took in the set and could see the ring on Evie's finger. It also took care of one for him. It wasn't so plain as to go unnoticed, and it was pretty in an economical way that fit with his bank account.

"That's so cute and simple," Charlie said, and he didn't want to think on that too closely.

"There's a matching engagement ring with this set, a stunning princess with round-cut diamonds." The jeweler pulled out a beautiful ring with a somewhat larger center stone and several diamonds on the band.

Danny didn't touch it, but Charlie did, reaching for the overpriced diamond after the jeweller slipped it onto the glass. She slid it on her ring finger and held it up in the light toward the door. There were people walking past, and he was feeling a little uncertain with Charlie there, considering it was only a few days ago he'd been dating her. It should have been awkward.

She smiled over at him. "I can see this on Evie, and the price is good, Danny. You should get this for her, because even though Evie is very plain and down to earth, this is something a guy should give the woman he's going to marry." Charlie then slid it off her finger.

He considered what she'd said, adding up the cost of the set, knowing it would put a dent in his account, but this was for Evie.

Charlie leaned in and kissed his cheek, holding the ring out to him. "Evie is a lucky woman, Danny."

He reached for the ring and then watched as Charlie started to the door. "You're leaving. Didn't you come in here for something?" he said.

She faced him, slipping on her shades, but she didn't smile. "I came in because I saw you walking past."

He didn't know what to say.

"I hope you're happy, Danny," she said. "I hope Evie is the one who makes you happy."

Then she pushed open the door and stepped out without a glance back to him, and he took in the matching set on the counter and the man who seemed overly interested and taken with Charlie.

"I'll take them both," he said.

Chapter Twenty-One

Danny had left Evie a hundred dollars in cash to pick up groceries, and Diana had loaned her the use of her SUV so Evie could make a trip into town, considering Danny had slipped over to his parents' the night before and come back with two plates of chili and some cornbread after showing her that he didn't have anything for them to eat. Not only did she get groceries, but she stopped at her parents' and picked up the boxes of personal items she'd already packed up the night before.

"You should wait for Danny and let him help you bring everything over," said Jed, her future father-in-law, as he followed her up the steps to the loft with her two boxes of things, mostly memorabilia she didn't need but wasn't about to part with. Jed had just been coming out of the barn when she pulled in. He was a man who didn't stand around and wait for a woman to carry anything. He had the same charm and quality she loved about Danny.

Evie carried the bag of groceries. Fortunately for

Danny, she was a damn good cook, considering she'd learned everything about meat from her father. All the side dishes, too, were something he'd taught her. "It's only a few things, and this way they're here," she said and set the grocery bag on the table.

Jed rested the boxes behind the sofa on the floor and then looked around at the neat and tidy loft. She noticed the hint of a smile that touched his lips. She could see so much of Danny in his father. "Can see you're already cleaning up after Danny, too. You'll have this no-frills bachelor pad turned into a home in no time."

What could she say? She was neat and tidy, and Danny wasn't. Although he wasn't a complete slob, he also had no interest in cleaning a house, decorating, or adding those simple touches that changed it from a place to sleep to a home. "Well, it's got to be done, and I have time. I want it to be nice for us, our first place together," she said, feeling shy.

Being there all day had given her time to think, to plan, to consider the changes she could make. Her truck was still parked, unmoving, outside the barn, and Danny had picked her up before he went to school and hadn't taken her home until he ran out of arguments to convince her to stay. It wasn't that she didn't want to stay and move in now; the fact was there was nothing Evie wanted more than to spend the night with Danny and start their future together. Neither was she old fashioned, because in her mind, there was nothing wrong with living together. It was more that she couldn't explain her need to wait the week, wanting everything to be perfect. Even her mom had asked why she wasn't living with Danny now.

Jed gestured to the grocery bag. "So I guess you'll be feeding him, too."

Evie unpacked two steaks, which had been on sale for cheaper than ground beef, along with vegetables, potatoes, oil, and citrus she could use for a marinade. She'd picked up enough essentials along with bread, cheese, and a few other necessities for the kitchen, and the other bag was still sitting in the back of the SUV, but at least she could start dinner. There would be lunch here, and Danny could have breakfast.

"I will, so you don't need to feed me and Danny for dinner tonight. Thanks again, Mr. Friessen," she said.

He shook his head and started toward her. "Jed. We're family now, or we will be soon…"

She heard Danny's Bronco. The way he pulled in was like his calling card, so much so that she had to fight to keep the grin from her face. She was dying to race down the steps and throw herself into his arms.

"And there he is," Jed added, his hand on the railing, and he started down the steps first.

Evie followed with the keys to the SUV. "Oh, here, before I forget, and thank Diana for me," she said at the bottom, handing Jed the keys.

Jed passed his son, who stepped out of the Bronco parked in front of the barn, and said something she couldn't make out as she waited. Jed kept going to the main house, whereas Danny stepped into the barn and slid his arms around her, pulling her closer, forcing her up to her tiptoes as he kissed her long and deep. She felt it all the way to her toes. She sighed when he pulled back, but he didn't let go of her.

"So I have groceries in the SUV and picked up

dinner so you don't need to run over to your parents' again tonight to feed us," she said.

He pulled back, and she took in his expression. It was priceless. Then she saw what looked like lipstick or something on the side of his jaw.

"What is that?" she said and brushed at what she thought was an off shade of red.

"What?" he said.

She showed him her finger. "You've been letting someone kiss you?" she teased, but as soon as she saw his face, his expression, it felt for a moment as if she'd been sucker punched.

"No, Evie, it's nothing like that. I just ran into Charlie, and…" He stopped talking, and she felt every muscle inside of her tighten.

"And, what, you just let her kiss you? Have you been spending time with her? Were you even going to mention it?" She didn't like the way this was making her feel, and she stepped back as he rubbed at where the lipstick had been. For a moment, he seemed angry, as if he had any right.

"Don't make this into something it isn't, Evie. I picked you, not Charlie, and it really is that simple. I ran into her, or rather she ran into me, and we were talking about you, and she kissed my cheek. I don't know why, and I certainly didn't kiss her. I wouldn't do that. There's nothing between us."

She knew Danny well, and she knew he wasn't dishonest, so why was she suddenly hit with a jealous feeling she didn't much like? It wasn't logical, yet there she was, feeling as if someone had encroached on her territory. Didn't he get that? She crossed her arms over her middle, and he held out his hand.

"Evie, come on."

She took a breath. "So why were you talking about me?" she asked.

Danny went silent, and she couldn't shake the hurt that came out of nowhere at the idea that he was sharing something with another woman. "It's…nothing," he said, and the way he hesitated had her fisting her hands and stepping back again.

"Well, I beg to differ. It is something, and it sounds like you don't want to share it with me but are choosing to share it with another woman—one, I might add, you were kissing a few days ago." Okay, she hadn't meant to say that, and she took in the dark look Danny leveled her way.

She could see past Danny to Diana and Jed in the distance, who were both out on the front deck, looking their way. Of course, they'd heard. She'd shouted it.

"Evie, you're being ridiculous and over-reacting…" Danny started.

Evie moved around him. Where she was going, she didn't have a clue. She took in her truck and Diana's SUV, realizing her purse was still sitting inside it along with the second bag of groceries. She felt his hand reach for hers, pulling her to a stop, and she wanted to slug him. Maybe he anticipated it, as he suddenly picked her up and tossed her over his shoulder.

"Put me down!" She was mortified and could feel his parents watching.

"Danny, put Evie down!" his mom called out.

"Danny!" Jed yelled, but Danny kept walking into the barn, turning once to them.

"She's fine," he called out. His hand was on her ass.

"Danny, put me down. This is ridiculous. Please," she said, feeling her face burn.

He started up the stairs and set her down, the back of her legs brushing the bed. "Evie, you need to hear me out. I love you, and I'm not sneaking around on you or meeting up with Charlie. I was working on a surprise for you when Charlie showed up. That's all, I swear. I'm not secretly meeting with her, seeing her. She isn't who I want. I thought you knew that. I asked you to marry me, I didn't ask Charlie, and I don't know what else to say to convince you, but don't walk away angry and think I've done something…"

She reached out and pressed her hand to his chest, and he stopped talking. She could feel how worked up he was and the passion that oozed from him. Then his hands were on her and pulling her closer, sliding up her arms until she was against him. He leaned down and pressed his forehead to hers, pressed a kiss to her lips, and she took another breath, connecting with him.

"Say something," he said as she fisted her hands into his shirt, loving the feel of being this close to him.

"So is this the kind of thing I can look forward to, you going all cave man on me?" she said.

He laughed and slid his palms over her cheeks, looking at her with those intense blue eyes that she swore she could get lost in forever. At the same time, she knew he only had eyes for her. "Yeah, when you won't see reason, so how about we practice the age-old art of making up?" He leaned in to kiss her, and she pressed her hand to his chest when his lips were just inches from her, feeling the warmth.

"I like that idea, but the wedding is just days away, and, Danny…" She slid her arms around his neck, feeling every hard part of him press into her. "I really want to wait until our wedding. I know that seems odd, and old fashioned, but please…" She pressed a kiss to his lips, feeling him stir. Then he stepped back, and she felt oddly cold, wanting him.

He ran a hand over his hair, letting out a rough laugh. "You really want to wait?"

For a minute, she wanted to say no as she took in this man she'd known forever. Then he shook his head, stepping back again before reaching into his pocket and pulling out a small box. He flipped it open, and she just stared at the gorgeous ring. She had to remind herself to breathe, pressing her hand to her chest.

"This is what I was buying for you," he said and lifted the ring from the box. He reached for her hand and slid it on her finger.

"Danny, it's so beautiful," she said as she looked up into his eyes, and the way he was looking back at her, there was so much there.

"I was in the jewellery store when Charlie walked in, buying this for you," he said. "Yes, she saw what I was buying, and the kiss was for us and our happiness, that's all. This ring is for you. I wanted you to have the one thing I didn't have to give you when I asked you to marry me."

Feeling the ring on her finger made everything so real, including how much she loved Danny. "Maybe I was too hasty. Maybe…" she started, and he just stared at her hard, the look almost pained. He stepped back again and this time started to the stairs. "Where are you going?" she asked as he walked another two steps down.

"Being the strong one, you want to wait, so we'll wait, even though it will likely kill me," he said. "I better tell my mom and dad that I haven't totally lost my mind and that you're safe and sound." He stopped at the bottom and looked back up to her, and for a moment, what he said in that one look meant more than words. It was the first time in her life that she felt absolutely, and deeply, loved.

Chapter Twenty-Two

Her dress was sleeveless, and the long flowing gown made her look and feel like a princess. It was the dress both her mom and Diana had insisted on after shopping all day in Arlington five days earlier.

She took in the loft that would be her and Danny's new home for the next few months, anyway. It was beginning to look like a home, with all the feminine touches, the photos, the flowers, the throw pillows, and a rug. Her image stared back at her in the full-length mirror beside the armoire, where her clothes were hanging with Danny's, and it had her breath catching in her throat. She'd never known herself to be anything other than average, but she was beautiful. Her brown hair was hanging in soft waves past her shoulders. The lace of her gown and the cut of her dress accentuated her small breasts, her slim waist, and the pearls in her ears turned the image to simple elegance. Even her mud-brown eyes, which she'd never really liked, dazzled with the makeup applied by her sister Sky.

"You ready? Oh my God, you're so beautiful!" said

Paige, her other sister, who appeared on the stairs. She was in a peach dress that was both tasteful and classy, her dark hair highlighted with blond. Sky followed in a dark blue sleeveless dress, her hair long and auburn with the help of a bottle of Clairol. She too seemed bursting with confidence.

"Thank you," Evie said, hearing voices outside. She knew it was Jed's family, friends from the area, and her family. Only a hundred, a small group, she realized, once Diana and her mother had finished with the list.

"Dad's waiting downstairs, and I hear Danny has asked twice if you're coming," Sky said with a giggle. "I even teased him that you could be having second thoughts and if any more time passes, it's likely you slipped out the back way." Sky did have a twisted sense of humor at times.

Evie took the small bouquet of mixed daisies that her sister had brought and started down the stairs on heels she wasn't used to wearing, gripping the railing. Her dad was waiting at the bottom, looking dashing in a black suit, a carnation pinned to his lapel and his dark hair freshly cut.

"You look beautiful," he said, holding his arm out. She took in the horses, whose heads were hanging over the stalls as if they were watching her. It was perfect.

"Thank you," she said as Sky lifted and straightened her long and flowing dress.

Evie started out of the barn on her father's arm. The sun was shining, and the cars were parked orderly off to the side. The yard in front of the house had been transformed with seven rows of white chairs, and everyone was now standing as Sky and Paige started walking ahead of her down the aisle, which led to the front deck, where Danny was standing. He looked so handsome, and the moment she saw him watching her, she couldn't pull her eyes away.

Her dad walked her up the aisle and to the steps, and he stopped at the bottom, kissed her cheek, and said to her, "Are you sure? It's not too late until you say 'I do.'"

She took a glance over to Danny and back to her father. "Yeah, I'm sure," she said.

Then Danny was holding out his hand, and she slipped hers into it as she lifted the front of her dress to walk up before the minister who was there to marry them. "Wow, look at you," Danny said, and he leaned in and kissed her.

The minister cleared his throat, and one of the men shouted out, "Wrong order, Danny! You've got to marry her first."

Everyone laughed. Danny just shook his head as he looked out at the crowd of people she hadn't been able to focus on.

The minister started, and Evie only half listened as she stood facing Danny, holding his hands, looking into his eyes, his face, his expression, and the love she knew was for her. He repeated his vows to her, promising to love, honor, and protect her. He squeezed her hand, and she had to fight the tears that threatened to erupt. She didn't know how she got the words out, as the entire ceremony seemed surreal, and then the minister asked for the rings. How could she have forgotten? Maybe her fear was there in her face, as Danny said, "I have the rings, all of them."

She took in the set, matching pink gold with simple diamonds on the band, as he slipped one on her finger.

His was in the same pink gold, which she couldn't believe he'd picked out, and she then slid it on his finger. His and hers. "You picked these out? Danny, they're so beautiful," she said.

He slid his hand over her cheek as the minister said, "Now you can kiss the bride, since you are man and wife."

She heard catcalling and cheers, and Danny pulled her close, his lips sliding over hers, kissing her deeply. Then he held her hand and walked her down the steps, and she was hugged and kissed by her mom and dad, Jed and Diana, and friends and family she'd never met. She felt as if she was in a fairytale.

The party was in full swing. Jed and Diana had brought in a local band, and her Dad had cooked up a barbecue along with wine and beer. There was dancing and laughing, and she didn't think anything could be more perfect, even when Danny pulled her into his arms to the middle of the dance floor, just a flat place in the dirt, and she swayed in his arms. When the sun went down, lanterns were hung, and the party continued.

Danny led Evie away.

"Where are we going?" she said. She couldn't stop laughing, and she couldn't stop looking at her ring as joy continued to bubble up in her.

"Upstairs. Let everyone else party, but you and I… I've got plans." Danny scooped her into his arms, and she squealed as she looped hers around his neck. "Shh," he said, smiling.

He was so damn handsome, and she couldn't believe this was happening as he carried her through the open door and reached back to lock it with a new deadbolt.

"Just in case, so no one tries to just walk in," he said, and then he started up the steps.

"You know you don't have to carry me up the stairs." She was giggling, and she couldn't believe it, as she didn't giggle.

He set her down beside the bed, his hand on her cheek, running over her shoulder and down her arm, and she shivered because the moment she'd waited for so long for was here. She hadn't even realized she'd been wanting him.

"You know what I've waited for," he said as he turned her around and undid the buttons along the back of her dress, then pulled at the zipper. His hands were on her shoulders as she felt the air brush her skin. He pulled the fabric apart, and it slid off her shoulders, to her waist. Danny pushed it down until the gown slid to the ground, where she stepped out of it in nothing more than lacy underwear and garters held up by stockings, something else that both her mother and Diana had insisted was a must-have.

She was still in her strappy sandals, and as Danny turned her around and allowed his gaze to take in all of her, from her small breasts to her toes, he didn't try to hide the appreciation.

"I think I could get used to this," he said as he lifted his hand and allowed the back of his fingers to brush over her shoulder, around her breast, and lower.

She pressed her hand against his chest, over his white shirt and open black suit jacket, and lower, to his waist, over the slim belt.

All of a sudden, he scooped her up and had her on the bed as he shrugged out of his jacket and pulled at his tie before tossing it free. He unbuttoned his shirt and pulled it from his pants, then dropped it to the ground before he joined her on the bed, pressing her into the mattress, allowing his hands to skim over her as if he were burning to memory every curve of her body. Then he kissed her again, this time taking her deep, tasting her as her hands pulled at his back. He kissed the curve of her neck, the crevice between her breasts, and her navel and her stomach, and ran his hands over her legs, lifting one and taking his time to appreciate the slenderness right down to her heel.

It was the shoes, she'd have to remember. He pulled them off along with the garters and her underwear, then stepped back and unfastened his belt, kicked off his dress shoes, and pulled off the rest of his clothes. Her eyes widened at how ready he was for her, and he stepped closer to the bed. In that second, she understood everything that was unspoken as he hovered over her, taking her in again as if he couldn't get enough. It seemed like forever, teasing, and she wanted him now.

She reached for him. "Please, Danny," she said and was stunned at the sound of her voice. It sounded strange, as if she were out of breath.

He pulled open the bedside drawer to find a condom and covered himself. Maybe it was the expression on her face that had him saying, "No kids yet, Evie. We have time for that down the road."

Then he lowered himself on her and kissed her again, deeply, and she thought for a moment she was living her dream, feeling Danny on her, skin to skin, her legs wrapping with his. Her hands ran freely over his back, feeling the muscles pull over his amazing ass as his hands brushed her thighs, and he was between them.

She moved with him. It was a moment in time when

they became one. She was feeling his breath, his heart-beat, realizing then that it was just them, Danny and Evie, in this room in the loft while the rest of the party continued outside without them. Evie knew then, as the world as she knew it exploded around them, that a lifetime with Danny was what she'd been meant for.

Chapter Twenty-Three

They had been married now for three months. He'd woken every morning with her softness pressed against him, loving her body, loving Evie, enjoying every moment of the time he had with her.

"So this is the last of it," Evie said as she carried a bag containing a potted deep purple aster, a gift from his mom.

The entire back of the Bronco was packed with boxes, pillows, luggage, and everything they needed to start a new life in Seattle.

"Well, no room back here. It'll have to ride up front," Danny said as he closed the back of the Bronco, taking in the glow on Evie's round face. Her eyes seemed to light up every time she was with him. He lifted his hand to her cheek, her chin, and then leaned down and pressed a kiss to her lips. He pulled back and took in the way her tongue darted out to taste where he'd kissed her. It was that simple moment that meant everything to him.

"So are you sure you have everything?" Diana asked. She seemed to have lines pulling at the sides of her eyes, dressed in faded jeans and a blue and green tank top, her hair pulled back in a ponytail. His dad was wearing his cowboy hat as he stepped up behind her, resting his hands on her shoulders as if he knew how tense she was.

"Mom, we have everything and then some. I have no more room in the Bronco for anything else, and remember, I told you, it's a small place." He glanced to Evie as she slid her hand over his arm and leaned against him. A smile tugged at her lips.

"So you'll call—often," his mom said, as if he could forget. His dad now stood right behind her, both his hands pressing into her shoulders as if supporting her. Danny could see how upset his mom was, and his dad obviously knew, as he just stood there, touching her, being there for her.

"Mom, we will call. We're not that far away. We'll come back and visit on weekends, when we can." He glanced to Evie again, knowing she'd picked up a waitressing job at a pub a block from the small furnished apartment they'd rented. He too was going to pick up something part-time that worked around law school.

His mom hugged Evie and kissed her on the cheek, and then she hugged him, and he was sure she was fighting tears as he wrapped his arms around her. He loved her deeply. There was something in his dad's expression, as if he too was fighting the emotion of the moment.

Danny patted his mom's back. "Mom, come on. It's okay. It's not as if I'm going away forever. Evie and I will be back, and law school is only…"

"Too long," she interrupted and stepped back, wiping away the dampness in her eyes, "but I'm proud of you."

His dad stepped around her and pulled Danny close, hugging him. "You look after your wife," he said, patting his back. Then he stepped back, leaned down, and hugged Evie. "You two better get going while you have daylight."

Jed pulled Diana close just as Mark and Christopher, with his unruly red hair and scruffy face, since he preferred not shaving, appeared. Neither said a word, as they'd already said their goodbyes, the kind brothers did at their age. "See ya!" That was it.

Danny walked Evie around the Bronco and watched as she climbed in the passenger side, the window rolled down in the last of the summer heat. She slid her hand over his arm, which rested there a second, and then he leaned in and kissed her again before he walked around the truck, taking in his parents, his brothers. In that moment, it seemed as if when they drove away and out of there, nothing would ever be the same.

As he slid behind the wheel, started his Bronco, and drove away, feeling a giant lump in his chest, he fought the urge to glance back in the rear-view mirror, instead keeping his eyes on the road ahead. Evie reached over and slid her hand over his thigh without a word. He realized this beginning wasn't just his but also Evie's. He was starting his new life now with the woman he loved, his wife.

Instead of saying anything, he lowered his hand and pressed it over hers where it rested on his leg just as he came to the highway, and then he turned right, pulling out. They both glanced back, seeing the house in the distance, the barn, the place he'd been born and grown up in and was now leaving. In that one touch, they said everything words couldn't.

Turn the page for a sneak peek of
IN THE CHARM the next book in *THE FRIESSENS*
Available in print, eBook and audio

Join a brand new generation of Friessens in *New York Times* and *USA Today* bestselling author Lorhainne Eckhart's Friessen Family series. In the latest volume, **Chris is used to having whatever he wants—but this time, the irresistible could come at a high price.**

When stubbornly independent Chris Friessen decides to pack up and travel the country on the back of his Harley, he doesn't expect that his decision to see the "real USA" will cost him in ways he can't imagine. He soon finds himself face down on some backroad, cuffed by small-town cops. To make matters worse, he's told to keep moving, but when he meets the incredibly sexy daughter of the sheriff, Chris can't resist doing exactly the opposite—even after realizing that the sheriff's deputy is head over heels in love with her.

JD is the daughter of a South Dakota small-town sheriff, teased by locals that if she were ever to consider marrying, she'd have a line of suitors around the block. But she's not interested, as the only man she's ever loved up and left, and her father was behind it. When she drives up on her father and his deputy toying with the extremely attractive redheaded Chris Friessen, she can't resist tossing him an invitation to dinner, and she never expects that he'll take her up on it.

Now, Chris may find that the irresistible JD comes with a lot more than he's bargained for.

In the Charm

CHAPTER 1

Of all the decisions twenty-three-year-old Chris Friessen had made, his latest was likely to cost him in ways he hadn't even begun to imagine, considering the flashing sheriff's lights in his side mirrors. The car had ridden up on his ass until he'd pulled over, and he was now parked on a road—scratch that, a secondary highway in the middle of nowhere.

Actually, it wasn't really nowhere. He'd covered roughly two hundred and twenty miles that day, with the heat and sun beating down, but he couldn't rightly pinpoint exactly which county or, for that matter, state he was in. He'd pulled off the main highway crossing the country from east to west, and now he was having a hard time remembering whether he was in one of the Dakotas or in Montana, which, in his mind, put him in the middle of nowhere.

"Turn off the bike and step off! Show me your hands." The deep voice of what sounded like one pissed-off cop boomed over the loudspeaker, but the twang did little to help Chris figure out exactly where he was.

He turned off his bike and kicked the support stand, then lifted his leg over slowly and stepped down, his hands going right to the strap of his helmet to lift it off.

"I said show me your hands, asshole!" the cop yelled, and the way he did so shot a bolt of fear straight through Chris.

His hands, suddenly with a mind of their own, jabbed in the air high enough that there could be no mistake he was following instructions to a T. His heart was hammering, feeling the heat of the approaching cop. He could just make out his feet scraping the pavement, and he was straining to hear everything through his thick helmet—the radio, the tick of something, and the wind that did little to cool off this scorcher of a day. He wanted to explain to this cop that he was…what, a great guy just seeing the country, travelling from state to state? Why had he been pulled over?

"If you'll just let me take off my helmet—" He didn't get to finish, because rough hands gripped his left wrist, and metal cuffs were slapped on as his other arm was twisted back roughly. The pinch of the metal shot through his arm. "Ah, fuck, what the hell?" he yelled from the sudden bite. Then his helmet was pulled off and dumped on the asphalt. The smash was instant as he saw the visor crack. There went two hundred and fifty dollars—and it had been on sale.

"You watch your mouth," the cop snapped. Then Chris was down on the ground, face down, feeling the heat from the midday sun on the blacktop and burning into him through the black leather jacket he always wore on his bike.

It wasn't just any bike, though. He turned his head, taking in his Harley, a Forty-Eight Special with a long wheel base that screamed badass class. Chris had fallen in love with it the moment he'd seen it through the window of the Arlington bike shop. Another cop was unfastening the gear tied on the back of the bike and going through the compartment where his wallet, ID, insurance, and everything of value were stashed.

"You mind telling me why you pulled me over?" Chris said, turning his head back to the side.

The cop who'd cuffed him and put him on the ground was in a black uniform shirt with a badge pinned to his chest. He was wearing dark shades and was a lot rounder in the middle, and he worked a piece of gum as he holstered his weapon and then leaned down to Chris. "You packing? Got any weapons on you?"

Rough hands patted him down, grabbing him in places no stranger had.

"No," Chris said. "Now how about answering my question? Why did you pull me over?" He was sure he hadn't been speeding. He was seeing the back country that everyone missed while taking the main roads that got them where they were going faster. Not Chris. No, in all his wisdom, he'd thought taking the backroads and seeing all the small towns and counties no one ever stopped in was the best way to see this country. Not one of his smarter choices, he realized now.

The cop said nothing, and Chris had to strain his neck to see him looking over to the other cop, who handed over Chris's license with a scowl.

"Seriously, guys, don't think I don't know what my

rights are. Why exactly am I cuffed and on the ground in the middle of nowhere?"

That was something his mother, Diana Friessen, a lawyer, had shared with him growing up, and he was thankful for it now. The knowledge of what exactly his rights were had kicked in. His brother Danny, who was just finishing up law school, had also shared with Chris all the ins and outs of the law and how rights were often violated, especially the rights of those who didn't have a clue what their rights were.

Chris knew, though. They had to have a reason to pull him over and cuff him, and then there was the really big one: They hadn't even read him his rights.

"Christopher Friessen, from North Lakewood in Washington," the cop drawled. "You're a long way from home." He held up Chris's registration and insurance, or so it seemed, from the papers he was holding. It was beginning to seem more and more that this was a fishing expedition—but for what, he didn't have a clue. Something he didn't think he was going to like.

"The name's Chris," he snapped. No one called him Christopher except for his mother—and his dad, grandparents, aunts, uncles, and brothers, Danny and Mark, but only when they wanted to push all his buttons. His brothers knew the effort he was making to get everyone to cut it out and stop calling him something he didn't see himself as. It was a baby name, a little kid's name, which didn't fit badass Chris, who rode a Harley and had saved up to travel the country and really see it instead of reading about it.

"You're a long way from home, there, Christopher. Mind telling me what you're doing out this way?"

Seriously, what the fuck? He had to bite the words back, hating this feeling of being toyed with. "The name's Chris, I already told you, and I'm just passing through. Didn't think that was a crime. Now how about uncuffing me and telling me why the fuck you're treating me like some criminal?"

He realized as soon as the words were out of his mouth that it had likely been the wrong thing to say. He turned his head right and then left, seeing both their badges pinned to their chests. The cop by his bike wasn't as old as the one who had pinned him down on the ground and cuffed him. He was dark haired wearing a hat, tall, and the way he stared down, unsmiling, his face seemed made of granite. Chris realized this was a lawman whose gun he'd never want to find himself on the wrong side of, considering the dark, completely unimpressed expression that stared him down.

"How about you settle on down there, boy, and mind your manners," said the other cop as his booted foot kicked Chris in the shin. He was older, with a deeper voice and a potbelly.

Chris had to turn his head to the side again as he took him in. He wore a ball cap over what Chris thought was a bald head. He appeared older, maybe his dad's age, he thought just as he spotted a car coming up behind them. It was a rusty color, an older-model import, from the looks of it, and it slowed as the older cop stepped out and lifted his hand. Chris couldn't see much as the car stopped just behind him and the cop leaned in the window.

"Hey there, baby girl. What're you doing out this way?"

The way the cop's voice changed from asshole to sappy had Chris wanting to roll his eyes. For a second, he considered calling out to the driver to...what, help him out of his predicament?

"Just finished delivering meals to some of the shut-ins and was heading home. Could ask you the same, Daddy. What're you doing all the way out here, and what did that man do?" Her voice was soft and sassy, and Chris wished he could see her face over the rusty fender and the bald tires, which were the only things in his view.

"Oh, that's nothing for you to worry your pretty little head about. Just a routine traffic stop."

Routine, his ass! There was nothing routine about this stop or the fact that he was cuffed, lying face down on the burning pavement in what, he was sure, was the ninety-degree heat of this late afternoon in early August.

"If this is just routine, then how about uncuffing me and letting me up?" he snapped.

Rough hands suddenly gripped his arm and pulled him up, and he had to stifle a groan at his wrenched shoulder. He took in the babe in the car. She had long dirty-blond hair and a killer smile—a knockout, from what he could see ten feet from the car with the wind-shield between them. He felt relief as the cuff loosened and he was suddenly free.

On instinct, he reached for his wrist and rubbed, rolling his shoulders. He couldn't imagine how anyone could spend hours with their arms cuffed that way. He couldn't see the eyes of the younger cop who'd uncuffed him from behind his shades as he stepped away from Chris and over to the car, lifting his hand and smiling at the killer babe.

"Hey there, JD," he said. "I'm sure the good folks of Martin appreciate all the help you're giving." The way his voice changed to overly affectionate was ridiculous.

"Ah, thanks, Ray. Just doing my part, is all. We have a lot of seniors who just can't get out anymore." She had a brilliant smile, and the cop actually touched his fingers to his hat and smiled brightly. It was one of those smiles guys did when they liked a girl, but Chris figured the guy had to be at least ten years her senior.

The balding cop tapped her open window. "You'd best get going, JD—and did you have a chance to talk to your mother yet?"

Chris wondered whether Daddy here had any idea his partner had the hots for his daughter. At the same time, he realized neither of them were giving him the time of day now. Could he just pick up his wrecked helmet, climb on his bike, and drive away? Likely not, considering they still had his license and registration, and his gear, which had been tied to the back, was now on the side of the road.

He didn't hear what she said, but then the car started moving, rolling the ten feet toward him, where it stopped, the passenger window still open. "Hey there, don't let these two ruffle your feathers. They're both harmless…and should know better than to pull over a stranger just because!" She yelled the last part back, looking over her shoulder.

Chris took in the pair he'd been shitting bricks about moments before, who now appeared a lot less threatening.

"You should stop in Martin on your way through. Come on over to Lulu's. Dinner is on the house for your trouble. The name's JD," she added with that killer smile, and he could see a killer body, too, in the bucket seat behind the wheel. She was wearing a floral tank and cutoffs. Then she lifted her fingers in a wave and pulled away, and he stared at the back end of the car and then back to the cops, who still hadn't told him why they'd felt the need to scare the ever-living shit out of him and treat him like America's most wanted.

"Here's your ID," said Ray, the scowl now once again pasted on his face. He held out Chris's papers and license.

The older cop, who was already walking to the passenger side of the cop car, where the lights were still flashing, lifted his hand. "You have yourself a great day, you hear, and move yourself along."

Then they were both in the car, and as it drove away with one blast of the siren, he tucked his ID back in the compartment in his wallet and noted the logo, *Bennett County Sheriff's Department*. He leaned down and picked up his helmet, taking in the crack right down the center of the visor. The repairs would be a pain in the ass to see through. The helmet was a big-ticket item, and he wasn't too happy to dish out that kind of cash. He wanted nothing more than to give those two asshole cops the bill and make them pay it. Yeah, good luck there.

At least now he knew where he was: South Dakota, outside Martin, in the middle of nowhere. Then there was the gorgeous chick, the daughter of one of the asshole cops who'd pulled him over, and he realized that maybe he wasn't too willing to listen to their advice. After all, as his mom and dad had pointed out a time or two, there was a side of him that just couldn't resist stirring things up when the smarter course would be to walk away.

He stared at the crack on his visor, his gear on the ground, and figured, what the hell? Dinner sounded like a great idea.

About the Author

"Lorhainne Eckhart is one of my go to authors when I want a guaranteed good book. So many twists and turns, but also so much love and such a strong sense of family."

(Lora W., Reviewer)

New York Times & USA Today bestseller Lorhainne Eckhart writes Raw Relatable Real Romance is best known for her big family romances series, where "Morals and family are running themes. Danger, romance, and a drive to do what is right will see you glued to the page." As one fan calls her, she is the

"Queen of the family saga." (aherman) writing "the ups and downs of what goes on within a family but also with some suspense, angst and of course a bit of romance thrown in for good measure." Follow Lorhainne on Bookbub to receive alerts on New Releases and Sales and join her mailing list at LorhainneEckhart.com for her Monday Blog, books news, giveaways and FREE reads. With over 120 books, audiobooks, and multiple series published and available at all retailers now translated into six languages. She is a multiple recipient of the Readers' Favorite Award for Suspense and Romance, and lives in the Pacific Northwest on an island, is the mother of three, her oldest has autism and she is an advocate for never giving up on your dreams.

"Lorhainne Eckhart has this uncanny way of just hitting the spot every time with her books."

(Caroline L., Reviewer)

The O'Connells: *The O'Connells of Livingston, Montana are not your typical family. A riveting collection of stories surrounding the ups and downs of what goes on within a family but also with some suspense, angst and of course a bit of romance thrown in for good measure "I thought I loved the Friessens, but I absolutely adore the O'Connell's. Each and every book has totally different genres of stories but the one thing in common is how she is able to wrap it around the family which is the heart of each story." (C. Logue)*

The Friessens: *An emotional big family romance series, the Friessen family siblings find their relationships tested, lay their hearts on the line, and discover lasting love! "Lorhainne Eckhart is one of my go to authors when I want a guaranteed good book. So many twists and turns, but also so much love and such a strong sense of family." (Lora W., Reviewer)*

The Parker Sisters: *The Parker Sisters are a close-knit family, and like any other family they have their ups and downs. "Eckhart has crafted another intense family drama…The character development is outstanding, and the emotional investment is high…" (Aherman, Reviewer)*

The McCabe Brothers: *Join the five McCabe siblings on their journeys to the dark and dangerous side of love! An intense, exhilarating collection of romantic thrillers you won't want to miss. — "Eckhart has a new series that is definitely worth the read. The queen of the family saga started this series with a spin-off of her wildly successful Friessen series." From a Readers' Favorite award—winning author and "queen of the family saga" (Aherman)*

Lorhainne loves to hear from her readers! You can connect with me at:
www.LorhainneEckhart.com

lorhainneeckhart.le@gmail.com

Also by Lorhainne Eckhart

The Outsider Series
The Forgotten Child (Brad and Emily)
A Baby and a Wedding *(An Outsider Series Short)*
Fallen Hero (Andy, Jed, and Diana)
The Search *(An Outsider Series Short)*
The Awakening (Andy and Laura)
Secrets (Jed and Diana)
Runaway (Andy and Laura)
Overdue *(An Outsider Series Short)*
The Unexpected Storm (Neil and Candy)
The Wedding (Neil and Candy)

The Friessens: A New Beginning
The Deadline (Andy and Laura)
The Price to Love (Neil and Candy)
A Different Kind of Love (Brad and Emily)
A Vow of Love, A Friessen Family Christmas

The Friessens
The Reunion
The Bloodline (Andy & Laura)
The Promise (Diana & Jed)
The Business Plan (Neil & Candy)
The Decision (Brad & Emily)
First Love (Katy)
Family First
Leave the Light On
In the Moment

The Fallen O'Connell
The Return of the O'Connells
And The She Was Gone
The Stalker
The O'Connell Family Christmas
The Girl Next Door
Broken Promises
The Gatekeeper

The McCabe Brothers
Don't Stop Me (Vic)
Don't Catch Me (Chase)
Don't Run From Me (Aaron)
Don't Hide From Me (Luc)
Don't Leave Me (Claudia)
Out of Time

A Billy Jo McCabe Mystery
Nothing As it Seems
Hiding in Plain Sight
The Cold Case
The Trap
Above the Law
The Stranger at the Door
The Children
The Last Stand
The Charity

The Street Fighter
Finding Home

The Wilde Brothers
The One (Joe and Margaret)

The Honeymoon, A Wilde Brothers Short
Friendly Fire (Logan and Julia)
Not Quite Married, A Wilde Brothers Short
A Matter of Trust (Ben and Carrie)
The Reckoning, A Wilde Brothers Christmas
Traded (Jake)
Unforgiven (Samuel)
The Holiday Bride

Married in Montana
His Promise
Love's Promise
A Promise of Forever

The Parker Sisters
Thrill of the Chase
The Dating Game
Play Hard to Get
What We Can't Have
Go Your Own Way
A June Wedding

Kate & Walker
One Night
Edge of Night
Last Night

Walk the Right Road Series
The Choice
Lost and Found
Merkaba
Bounty
Blown Away: The Final Chapter

The Saved Series
Saved
Vanished
Captured

Single Titles
He Came Back
Loving Christine

For my German Readers
Die Außenseiter-Reihe
Der Vergessene Junge
Der Gefallene Held

For my French Readers
L'ENFANT OUBLIÉ

www.ingramcontent.com/pod-product-compliance
Lightning Source LLC
Chambersburg PA
CBHW030942210726
48290CB00007B/2299